HARRY STARKE

BLAIR HOWARD

HARRY STARKE

A Novel By

Blair Howard

Harry Starke

ISBN: 9798711567806

ACKNOWLEDGMENTS

I would like to thank my son-in-law, Hamp Johnston, for his financial advice and expertise. You are the man, Hamp.

1

It was just after midnight. The wind was howling through the ironwork, blowing in off the river, and it was snowing, almost a blizzard, small flakes flying fast, horizontal. I was cold. I pulled my collar up around my ears, leaned over the parapet, and stared down into the darkness. The lights from the aquarium and the Market Street Bridge sparkled on the surface of the water.

Whitecaps on a river? I remember thinking. *What the hell am I doing here?*

A good question, and one for which I had no good answer. I'd spent the hours before midnight at the Sorbonne, a fancy name for a dump of ill repute, one of Chattanooga's sleaziest bars. I frequented it more often than I probably should, mostly to keep an eye on the lowlifes that inhabit the place. It's what I do.

Yes, I'd had a couple of drinks. Yes, really, it *was* only two, and no, I wasn't drunk. If you want to know the truth, I was bored, bored out of my brains watching the drunken idiots hitting on women they didn't know were hookers. At first it was kind of funny, then just pathetic. Finally, I'd had enough. I left the Sorbonne a little before twelve. The company had been bad, the liquor terrible, and the music... well.... *How do they listen to that stuff?*

Late as it was, I wasn't ready to go home. So I figured I'd take a walk, wander the streets a little, then grab a cab and go to bed. It was a stupid thing to do. Chattanooga isn't the friendliest town at midnight in winter, but there I was on the Walnut Street Bridge, freezing my ass off, staring down into the water, and... I was a little nervous.

I wasn't worried I might get mugged. Far from it. I'm a big guy, an ex-cop, and I was carrying a concealed weapon in a shoulder rig under my left arm. But there was something in the air that night, something other than the driving snow, and I could feel it. Something I couldn't put my finger on. It made my skin crawl.

I'd walked the few yards north on Broad, turned right on Fifth, then left on Walnut, and from there to the bridge, a pedestrian-only walkway across the Tennessee River to North Shore.

I was still on the south side, on the second span, leaning on the parapet looking west along Riverfront Parkway. I must have been standing there shivering for more than thirty minutes when I saw her. Well, I heard her first. She was on Walnut, running toward me, her heels clicking on the sidewalk. I recognized her. I'd seen her earlier, in the Sorbonne. She'd been sitting at the bar with two men, two tough-looking creeps, one tall and black with slicked back hair, the other one not so black, better dressed, smaller, and obviously the alpha. They were both wearing those shiny, quilted jackets. I'd wondered at the time what the hell she was doing there with them. She was out of their league by a mile: a classy, good-looking woman who looked as if she'd be more at home at the country club than at Benny Hinkle's sleazy dive.

She was maybe twenty-six or twenty-seven years old and wearing one of those little black dresses that cling and stick to every curve. She had red hair. Not that gaudy, fiery orange kids seem to go for these days—a muted amber that was either her own or had cost more than most people earned in a week. But it was her face that grabbed you. She might have been right out of one of those glossy fashion mags, a face that could only have come from good breeding—wow, there's an old-fashioned term—and I remember thinking, *She's probably the wife or daughter of one of the movers and shakers up on the mountain.* Add the pair of four-inch black stilettoes and the white cashmere parka that could only have come from 5th Avenue or Rodeo Drive, and I knew immediately that she was no ordinary, working-class pickup.

So what's she doing here arguing with those two? I remember thinking. I also remembered how I shook my head and stared at her legs. They seemed to go all the way up to her ears, and then some.

But I didn't dwell on her for long. I was too wrapped up in my own workaday problems to give a damn, but there was something about her that caught my interest and wouldn't let go.

Now here she was in the wind and snow, running, frightened, looking back over her shoulder as if she were being chased. Then she tripped, stumbled, almost fell. I started toward her, but as soon as she saw me, she stopped. She put her hands to her mouth, looked desperately about her, then turned, ran to the rail, and started to climb.

"No!" I shouted as I sprinted the few yards that separated us, but I was too late. She was on the rail before I could reach her. She looked wildly around, first along Walnut and then at me... and then she jumped. I dove the last couple of yards, my arms outstretched, and managed to grab the collar of that fancy parka with both hands. I slammed into the rail. Man, she was heavy. I hung onto the fabric, hauled on it as hard as I could, but it wasn't enough. She simply threw her arms over her head, slipped out of it, and fell. I barely heard the splash over the noise of the wind howling through the ironwork overhead. I leaned over the rail and looked down. Nothing, just the white caps on the river some eighty feet below. She wouldn't last more than a few minutes in those icy waters, supposing she'd even survived the fall.

I took out my cell and dialed 911. There was nothing else I could do. I told the operator what had happened, gave her my name and location, and sat down on one of the bench seats to wait, the parka folded over my lap. I picked it up. It was heavy.

Okay, okay. I'm a nosy son of a bitch. But I'm a private detective, and the temptation was just too much. I searched the pockets. I didn't find much. There was a set of keys to a BMW in one, and a pair of white cashmere gloves and an iPhone 6 in the other. I pulled down the zipper at the front, looked at the tag and inside of the collar: Neiman Marcus. In the inside pocket found a leather clutch, pale blue, with a snap closure at the top. It was unusual, obviously expensive, and a little larger than those handy little accessories most trendy young women like to carry. I opened it and rifled through the contents. *Geez, $2,300 in hundreds, and God knows how much in fifties and twenties.*

I put the money back, fiddled some more, found three business cards—also expensive—and a key. An ordinary key, as far as I could tell. The cards read "Tabitha Willard." Her address? Her occupation? Nada. There was nothing on it other than the name and a phone number. I searched the purse and all of her pockets again, but again found no driver's license, no ID. *Keys to a Beemer, but no license. That's strange.*

By now, I could hear sirens, so I returned everything to the purse... well, everything except one of the cards, which I slipped into my own overcoat pocket, and returned the purse to the inside pocket of the parka.

"What the hell have you done now, Starke?"

I might have known. It took only my name and a 911 call to attract the attention of the CPD in general, and Sergeant Lonnie Guest in particular. That fat bastard hated my guts and didn't care who knew it. He had since we were at the police academy together. He couldn't get his head around how tough it had been for him, and how easy for me. I always wondered how he'd made it through at all, much less past the final exam. Then I found out: the SOB was a cousin to the mayor. Hah, even that didn't help him much. As soon as the cousin lost the election, Lonnie lost his support. He made sergeant eight years ago, just before the mayor left office. It was his honor's last official act, his way of getting back at the city for not supporting him. Lonnie's going nowhere in the department, has no chance of promotion. The dumbass can't pass the lieutenant's exam.

I looked up at him and smiled the smile I knew chapped his jaw.

"Not a thing, Lonnie. I just made the call. She went over the rail into the water. I managed to save her coat. Here you go." I tossed it to him. He caught it and scowled, first at the coat, then at me.

"You're trouble, Starke. Nothin' but trouble. You may

have the rest of 'em flimflammed, but not me. We shoulda locked you away years ago. Tell me what happened."

"Nah. I'll wait till someone who knows what they're doing gets here. No point in spilling it all twice."

"You'll tell me, you arrogant son of a bitch. I'm first officer on the scene."

"So you are, Lonnie, so you are. Is that soup you have on your shirt?"

He looked down. I laughed. "Gotcha."

"Screw you, Starke, you piece of shit."

I looked at my watch, took out my phone, texted Lieutenant Gazzara, and asked her to come on down. She would not be pleased.

"Suicide, Lonnie. She ran along Walnut like the devil was after her, spotted me, and hopped over the rail. Gone, Lonnie. Into the river. Suicide."

The phone vibrated in my pants pocket. I pulled it, unlocked it, and read the text.

"Now look, Lonnie, Kate Gazzara will be here in just a few, so why don't you go back to your cruiser where it's nice and warm, maybe take a nap, and I'll just hang out on this bench until she arrives."

"One of these days she ain't gonna be around to save your ass, Starke, an' I wanna be there when that happens."

"Yeah, well. In the meantime, you probably should make some calls, get some boats down there, and divers too. Not that they'll find anything in this mess." I looked up into the swirling snowstorm. It must have been blowing twenty miles an hour at least.

"Who the hell d'you think you are, Starke, givin' me orders? You just keep your trap shut and let us do our job, okay?" Then he did as he was told. He got on the phone and requested help from the Tennessee Wildlife river patrol and a dive team. Hah!

I grinned and settled down to wait, but not for long. She arrived less than five minutes later in an unmarked, and I was right; she didn't look happy.

"This had better be good, Harry, bringing me out in this weather. I'd been home less than ten minutes when you texted. I was on my way to bed." She sat down on the bench beside me.

I turned to look at her. She always amazed me. No matter what time of day or night, Kate always looked good: almost six feet tall, slender figure—ripped, I suppose is how you would describe it – she works out a lot. When she's at work, she keeps her long tawny hair tied back, but it was down just then, cascading around her shoulders, whipped by the wind. She has huge hazel eyes and a high forehead. She was wearing jeans tucked into high-heel boots that came almost up to her knees, and a white turtleneck sweater under a short, tan leather jacket. Even at one o'clock in the morning in the middle of a snowstorm, she looked stunning.

"So tell me what happened."

And I did. I told her the events of the past forty minutes, culminating with the girl taking a dive from the bridge. She didn't interrupt. She listened carefully to every word, nodding every now and then, and then she started asking questions.

"So, Harry...." She looked me in the eye. "Slumming again, huh? Why do you do it? Why do you go to places like the Sorbonne?"

"Just keeping my ear to the ground. It's in places like the Sorbonne where you learn things, not the fancy bars and restaurants."

"So... what did you find in her pockets?"

"Kate!" I tried to sound indignant, as if going through the woman's clothing was something I would never even think of doing, but she knows me better than I know myself. She tilted her head sideways and raised her eyebrows, an unspoken question.

"Okay," I sighed, and shook my head. "Yes, I glanced through her stuff." She rolled her eyes. "I hung onto this." I handed her the card. "There are two more just like it in her purse, wallet, whatever the hell it is. There's also a wad of cash, and a fob for a late-model BMW, the keyless type. No driver's license, though. Strange, huh?"

She nodded, fingered the card, turned it over, and looked at the back. "Hey! Sergeant Guest." She had to shout to be heard over the wind. "Bring that coat over here, will you please?"

Please? I'd have told the creep to get his fat ass over here, and quick, but I guess she's more lady than she is cop.... Nope, that ain't true. The lady's a lady, but she's all cop.

We both watched as the big sergeant leaned inside his cruiser and retrieved the parka. *Geez, am I glad I haven't just eaten.*

He backed out of the car, then sauntered over. You ever seen a fat guy saunter? It's hilarious. The look on his face was a treat to behold too, when he dropped the coat on her lap. He looked like he'd just bitten into a lemon.

"Might be a good idea to search this light-fingered piece of garbage while you're at it, LT," he said with a smirk. "There's a whole lot o' cash in the wallet. Some of it might o' stuck to Starke here." He nodded down at me. I grinned back up at him.

"That's enough of that talk, Sergeant. How long before Wildlife and the divers get here?"

"They're on their way. Shouldn't be too much longer. I'll go wait in the cruiser, if it's okay with you."

"Yeah, go on. I'll call if I need you." She waited until he was back inside his car before she handed me the card. "I didn't give you that. If anyone asks, you stole it, right?"

I nodded. "Kate, the girl was frightened out of her mind. She seemed fine when I saw her earlier in the bar with two nasty-looking creeps. What the hell could have scared her like that? And what was she doing with those two? I've seen them around, but I don't know who they are. She was a lovely kid, Kate. I want to know what happened."

She didn't answer. She got to her feet, unfolded the parka, and let out a low whistle. "Whoa, cashmere, Neiman Marcus. This little number must have set her back at least four grand, maybe more. What I wouldn't give for one of these." She tucked the coat under her arm and opened the clutch.

"How much money is in here, Harry?" She rifled through the wad of bills.

"I'm not sure."

"Twenty-three hundreds, along with nine fifties and eight twenties: $2,910 in all. That's a lot of cash to be carrying around loose, especially into a place like the Sorbonne. What could she have been thinking?"

I nodded, but I didn't say anything. The divers were arriving on Riverfront Parkway, and there were blue lights flashing on the river; Tennessee Wildlife was there, too.

"Okay, Harry. You'd better take off and go home. Oh, and, Harry, I know you're going to be looking into this; you can't help yourself. This time, though, that's probably a good thing, because we can't. It's a suicide, plain and simple; you said so yourself. We'll try to identify her, contact her next of kin, and... well, know how it goes. When we do, I'll call you, but you're right; from what you saw in the bar, there may be something more going on. If so, we need to know about it. That's on you, Harry. I'll help, if I can, but stay out of trouble, and keep that damn gun in its holster. One more incident like the last one, and I won't be able to save you. You got that?"

She was talking about something I'd done a couple of months ago. I had to pull my weapon on a suspect. Turned out the guy was innocent. He didn't press charges, but the police weren't too happy about it. It wasn't the first time they didn't like something I did, though, and it surely wouldn't be the last.

"Got it. I'll start first thing in the morning." I looked at my watch. "Damn, it already is morning."

"Harry, if you find anything, anything at all, call me, please. Otherwise, we'll stay in touch by text, right?"

I agreed. She folded the Neiman Marcus and walked slowly, head down, back to her car. As she passed Guest's patrol unit, she stopped, leaned in the window, and said something I didn't hear. Two minutes later, she hit the starter, did a three-point, sped off along Walnut, then turned left on East 4th, going east toward the hospital, going home, I supposed.

I didn't wait until morning. I walked off the bridge onto Walnut, then turned right and found a bench outside the aquarium. I took the card out of my pocket and punched the number into my phone.

"Yeah?" A male voice.

"Tabitha Willard, please?"

Click.

Son of a bitch. He hung up. I tried again, but there was no answer.

Okay, so it would have to wait until the city was awake. Bed seemed like a good idea.

I checked my watch. 1:15. I called a cab, then hunkered down in a doorway, out of the wind, and waited.

It was no more than a fifteen-minute ride to my place at that time in the morning. I paid the cabbie, slipped him an extra ten and wished him goodnight, what was left of it.

I threw my coat down on a chair in the kitchen, poured myself a stiff measure of Laphroaig Quarter Cask scotch and flung myself down on the sofa in front of the picture window. The wind and snow had slacked off almost to nothing, just a light breeze and a few flurries. A light mist covered the surface of the river, a soft gray blanket that swirled and undulated, turning the mighty Tennessee into a living thing. The view from my window was, as always, spectacular.

I lay there, staring out over the water, savoring the ten-year-old malt. My brain was in overdrive. The events of the past few hours came flooding back. Time after time, I saw the horrified look on the girl's face when she spotted me. I kept remembering the way she dropped, slowly turning end over end, splashing into the murky water far below. Was there anything else I could have done to save her? I was sure the question would haunt me for the rest of my days... and nights. There'd be no sleep for me that night.

Geez, what a way to go.

2

I woke to a bright, sunny morning... late, but still morning, the sound of my cell phone jangling in my ear. *Geez, already? I have to change that damned ring tone.*

"Starke."

"Harry, it's Kate. Where are you?"

"Still home. Why? What's up?"

"Still home? Do you know what time it is?"

"Er... no. You woke me up. I don't even know what day it is."

"Harry, it's Tuesday. It's almost eleven."

"Eleven? Damn. I overslept."

"We need to meet. I have some news."

I looked at my watch. "My office. Give me an hour. Noon? I'll buy you lunch."

"'Kay, see you then."

Damn! Eleven o'clock already. I'm going to have to quit with the booze... Nah.

I took one last look out over the river and hopped out of

bed. In the kitchen, I hit the go button on the coffee maker for a large cup of coffee, then went back to my bedroom, stripped, and took a long cold shower.

Ten minutes later I was dressed and on my way downtown.

I run a private investigation agency in Chattanooga, with a small suite of offices just a couple of blocks from the Flatiron Building on Georgia. It's close to the courts and law offices—a great location for what I do. I work for a whole range of clients, from lawyers to corporate entities to members of the general public

I employ a staff of nine, including five investigators, two secretaries, an intern, and my personal assistant, Jacque Hale.

I know just about everyone who matters, not only in Chattanooga, but also in Atlanta, Birmingham, and Nashville, not the least of whom is my old man. It's not what you know, but who you know, right?

My father, August Starke, is a lawyer, a very good one. He specializes in tort, which is a classy word for personal injury. You've probably seen him on TV. His ads run on most local stations almost every day. He made sure that I got the best education money could buy. I graduated McCallie in '91—and so did most of the movers and shakers in this city of ours; not all in '91 of course—and I have a Master's degree in Forensic Psychology from Fairleigh Dickinson.

My agency does a lot of work for my father. His latest claim to fame was his successful class action lawsuit against one of the big drug companies. He brought in millions in compensation for local victims of the birth control fiasco. Now he has his teeth into another case: some of the new high-tech blood thinners seem to be causing more problems than cures. We're doing some work for him on that one, too.

It was right at noon when I walked into my office. I'm not usually that late. I make it a habit to be at my desk no later than seven thirty. The rest of the crew is expected in no later than eight, unless they're on assignment.

Kate was already there when I arrived, seated in one of those leather chesterfield chairs that seem to be the obligatory norm in most professional offices. She was wearing jeans, a black sweater, and the same tan leather jacket she'd worn the night before. Her hair was pulled back and tied in a ponytail. She, and everyone else, looked up when I walked in. They all grinned.

"Okay, so I'm late, dammit."

I rolled my eyes, beckoned for Kate to follow me, and went into my inner sanctum. I waited until she'd seated herself, then I poked my head out the door, caught Mike's attention, pointed at the coffee pot, and raised two fingers.

Now, I have to tell you, there's really only one place where I'm truly happy, other than my condo, and that's my office. It's as comfortable as I could possibly make it. It has all the trimmings: the big desk, leather chairs, computer, and all, but I also spent a lot of money on the decor. The walls are paneled with dark walnut; there are two floor-to-ceiling bookshelves; the ceiling itself is painted a soft magnolia color; the carpet is pure wool—dark red. The window is covered with ivory sheers accented with heavy drapes that match the carpet. The artwork, a half-dozen pieces, is original—local scenes by local artists—not worth a fortune, but costly enough. There's also a small drinks cabinet where I keep my special goodies. The room had been designed by a master. Her intention was to instill in my clients a sense opulence and success, and I think she succeeded. Kate laughingly calls it my man cave.

I didn't take the seat behind my desk. Instead, I sat in the one next to Kate. Mike brought the coffee. Life was good.

Kate looked around the room. "Do you ever miss being a cop, Harry?"

"Nope. What about you? You need to get out of that rat race, too. Come work for me. You'll make more money."

"Hah, not a chance. And what the hell would you do without me on the inside if I did?"

"Good question. I'd work it out. Don't I always? So tell me: what about the girl?"

"They found her an hour after we left. I saw her this morning. What a damn shame."

I nodded, said nothing, and waited for her to continue.

"The name on the business card was correct. She is —*was*—Tabitha Willard. The phone number is disconnected."

"It wasn't at one o'clock this morning. I called it. A male answered. He hung up when I asked for her. Were you able to trace it?"

"Nope. It was probably a burner."

"That doesn't mean it can't be traced. They have to be activated, right?"

She nodded.

"That will tell us where it was purchased. If it came from one of the big stores, they usually have security cameras, and that means photos. Photos can be identified. I'll have Tim look into it."

She nodded again and sipped her coffee.

"How did you identify her?"

"Her prints are on file. Shoplifting. A year ago."

"So who is she? Where's she from? Geez, Kate. Don't make me drag it out of you."

"She's the daughter of Justin Willard. Ring any bells?"

"Not that I can think of. Who is he?"

"One of our best-loved plastic surgeons. If you need to get rid of the wrinkles? He's the man. Need new tits? He's the man. Need a new face? Well, you get the idea. He's been around a long time. Impeccable reputation. Rich as Croesus."

"That rich, huh? Okay. So, have you informed the family?"

"Oh yeah. I went up there myself, just before I came here. I also went and had a word with her sister Jessica and Charlotte Maxwell, Tabitha's best friend. And, by the way, I told the good doctor to expect you."

"Up there? Lookout, right?"

"Yep! It's on Cheatham Avenue. Nice place. Must be worth a couple of mil."

"So?"

"Hell, Harry, they hadn't even missed her. She lived in an apartment over the garage. Why would anyone want a six-car garage? It must have cost almost as much to build as the home. Harry, the man drives a Rolls Royce; he owns a damn jet, for God's sake."

"Hah, so does my father—own a jet, not a Rolls, and there are more than a few around here who own one of those, too. I think I'd like to have me one someday."

She looked at me; her expression was priceless.

"Joking, Kate. Joking. What did he say when you told him I was coming to see him?"

"He said for you to call first to make sure he was home. If not, he said you can go by his office. Other than that, he didn't seem bothered about you visiting. But maybe it didn't register. He *was* kind of upset." She leaned over the desk, grabbed a pen, and scribbled a number on the blotter. "That's his home number. He wouldn't give me his cell. His office number is in the book."

I nodded. "Okay, so tell me about Tabitha."

"There's not much to tell. They found her less than a hundred yards from the bridge. Her neck was broken, probably from the fall. She was wearing a black dress, no shoes—you said she was wearing some when she went over so we're assuming they came off in the water—a Rolex watch, a couple of gold bracelets, both eighteen karat, and—" she looked at me, and then continued: "no underwear."

I grinned at her. Nah, I smirked. "None?"

She rolled her eyes. "No, pervert, none at all. No bra, no panties, nothing."

"She may have lost the panties when she hit the water." I grinned at her. "I've lost my trunks more than once, making a splash."

"True. That could be it. She was also wearing this."

She handed me a thin gold chain with a pendant attached. The pendant was in the form of two serpents entwined, each swallowing the other's tail. It was quite small, not much bigger than a quarter. It was unique. I'd never seen anything like it before.

"What is it, Kate?"

"Search me. It's unusual, eighteen-caret gold, the chain, too, and expensive, like everything else about her. Her father said he hadn't seen it before, so did her sister and her friend, which I thought was strange.... Maybe you should check it out. Anyway, that's about all I've got. Now you know more than I do. Let's go get some lunch. Your treat."

"Sure, as always."

"Oh come *on*, Harry. You can afford it."

"That I can, but it would be nice if you offered, just once."

"Okay then. My treat. The Deli?"

I nodded. We both rose to our feet.

"Kate?"

"Yeah?"

"Can I borrow the pendant? Just for a day or two?"

She shook her head. "I'd rather not. It's valuable, and I'd be in serious trouble if you lost it."

I tilted my head sideways. "Okay, lemme get a picture of it then." She put it down on my desk, and I snapped a photo with my iPhone.

"That ought to do it. Let's go." I handed her the pendant, and we left the office.

"One more thing, Harry." She reached into her jacket pocket, bringing out the key she'd taken from the girl's pocket. "Here. Take it. I have no idea what it's for. Neither did the old man or her sister, or her friend. Maybe it means something. Maybe it doesn't. Give it some thought, okay?"

I nodded, slipped the key into the pocket of my jacket, and then followed her out onto the street. It's always nice to follow Kate. She has a great ass.

The Flatiron Deli is housed in the building that bears the same name, just a couple of blocks away from my office, very handy, and the food is good, too. They make the best BLT in town. I ordered one of those with a cup of coffee. Kate had a Muffaletta, a Coke, and a loaded baked potato to go with it.

How does she eat all those calories and keep the weight off?

We sat opposite each other in a booth. We ate quietly for a while, then we both spoke at once.

I smiled at her. "Ladies first."

"I was about to tell you that we found her car. It was parked in the multi-story near the aquarium. It was clean, Harry, and by clean I mean it had been wiped; it was spotless."

"Hmmm."

She nodded. "What about those two you saw her with in the bar? You said you've seen them before?"

I nodded and said, "I've seen them a couple of times. They were a weird pair. For some reason, they reminded me of Stimpy and Ren." She smiled at that. "One was a tall, well-built guy, black, with slicked back hair, arrogant. The smaller guy was clean shaven, lighter skinned, assertive. I got the feeling that he was running the show. I couldn't hear what they were talking about, but I could tell they were arguing. She was holding her own, though."

I looked at my watch. It was almost two o'clock.

"Kate, I think I'll head down that way, to the Sorbonne, see if I can get anything out of Benny Hinkle. He was running the bar last night. You done?"

She got up from the booth. "Good idea. Call me later. Let me know if you find anything. When do you expect to go see Willard?"

"I was thinking I'd head up that way early this evening. You wanna go?"

"Can't. Hot date. Don't forget to call him first." She leaned over, pecked me on the cheek, then walked quickly out of the Deli. You guessed it. She'd stiffed me for the tab, and the tip. I had to grin. She was a rare one. And then it hit me.

Hot date? What was that about? Kate never dates. Well, just me, I think.

I returned to my office, gave Tim the phone number on Tabitha Willard's card, and asked him to see if he could track it down. I made a couple of calls, then headed out again.

3

I parked my car next to a meter on Broad and walked the few blocks to the bar. The Sorbonne was dark inside. The sign on the door gave the hours as "4 pm until whenever." It wasn't a joke. It was still early afternoon. I looked at my watch. Two thirty. I walked to the end of the block, turned left into the alley, and then left again. The rear entrance was two doors on. I rang the bell.

I heard the sound of locks being turned. The door opened six inches and an eye appeared in the gap.

"Hello, Benny," I said, giving the door a shove. The door flew open and Benny staggered back, giving me enough room to slip in and then push the door shut.

"Whaddaya want, Starke? We ain't open for another two more hours."

Benny Hinkle is actually the owner of the Sorbonne. He's been running it for years. He's also known me for years —when I was still a cop. Oh yeah, he knew me all right. He never liked me, but then he never liked any cops. Now he likes me even less, mostly because he knows that now that

I've gone private, I don't have to follow the rules. He does, however, respect muscle and attitude. I have plenty of both, as he'd learned several times in the past, and much to his regret. He would have barred me from the Sorbonne, if he could, but he didn't have the balls to try it.

"I know that," I said. "I just want to ask a few questions."

He looked guardedly at me through shifty, half-closed eyes. "What questions? I don't know nothin' an' I wouldn't say if I did."

"Let's go and sit down somewhere comfortable, Benny. Your office, maybe?"

He hesitated, nodded, and then turned and walked a couple of steps, pushed open a door, and walked inside.

Geez, what a mess. How can anyone live and work like this?

The filthy, cluttered rat's nest included a variety of empty pizza boxes, a half-dozen of them stacked on top of a file cabinet. The desk was inches deep in papers, bills, delivery notes, newspapers, and what looked like the remains of at least two meals. There was an iron bed set against the wall under the window. The window was hung with rags that must have been curtains in the distant past. The place stank of cats; there were three of them curled up together on the unmade bed. At least a dozen beer crates, soft drink crates, and cardboard boxes full of empty wine and liquor bottles were stacked against the walls. The floor was littered with cat food, and the two litter boxes looked as if they hadn't been cleaned in a month.

The man's a frickin' pig.

"So, whaddaya want, Starke?"

Phuttt. The seat cushion almost exploded as he dropped

his fat ass down into the chair behind his desk. Seated, he ran his fingers through his greasy brown hair.

I sat down in the only other chair in the room, one of those steel-framed folding things.

"You been to bed yet, Benny? You look like shit."

"Yeah, well. I got lots to do, and no time to do it. I'll maybe take a nap when Laura gets here. Nothin' much happens till after ten, as you well know. Come on, Starke. Spill it. What do you want?"

"I was in the bar last night, Benny. Remember?"

He nodded. "How could I forget?"

"Do you remember the girl in the black dress and white coat?"

"Come on, Harry. There were lots of girls in here last night. You know that. You were here, for God's sake. The place was packed."

"Yeah, I was here. And so were you. This was around midnight. She had dark red hair and an expensive white coat. She was with a couple of brothers. Nasty-looking types."

"Oh yeah, I remember her. Who wouldn't? She was hot."

"Yeah, well, she's not so hot now. She's pretty cold. She's dead. What do you know about her?"

"Dead? Dead? How? I don't know nothin', not a thing. I ain't never seen her before. Who killed her?"

"Nobody killed her, Benny. She threw herself off the bridge. So. What about the brothers?"

"Killed herself, huh? Wow! Um...." He hesitated. "Nothing. I ain't never seen 'em before either." He looked away as he said it.

I said nothing. I just sat there and watched his face.

"What?" he said, when he had gathered up enough courage to look me in the eyes again.

"You're about as transparent as that window, Benny. Maybe more so. It's filthy. Now tell me the truth."

"Screw you, Starke. I don't have tell you nothin'. Get the hell out of my office, and stay outta the bar, too."

I sat there for a moment, contemplating his fat face, then I nodded and rose to my feet. But I didn't leave. I walked around the desk, reached inside my jacket, pulled my Smith & Wesson M&P9, and sat down on the desk facing him.

"Whoa." He leaned away from me, eyes wide, hands thrown up in front of him with his fingers spread.

"Now then, Benny. There are two ways we can do this," I said. "Either way, you'll tell me what I want to know. So, what do you think? Painful or not?"

"Harry, I swear I don't know those two guys. I barely even noticed 'em."

I nodded, and then tapped him gently on the bridge of his nose with the barrel of the gun.

"Ow, ow, ow," he yelled. "That hurt, you son of a bitch."

"I asked you, Benny... painful, or not? You chose painful." I tapped him again.

"Damn it, Harry. Quit it. You'll bust my nose."

"Yup, it's quite likely I will. You ready to talk?"

"I told ya, I don't know who they are."

Smack. This time I laid the flat side of the gun hard against his ear.

Hah, the man was actually crying, sobbing as he rubbed his ear. The bridge of his nose was already turning black.

I grabbed his right hand and slammed it down on the desktop, fingers spread.

"Benny, you want to talk to me before I start on your fingers?"

"Okay, okay." He nodded enthusiastically. "They—they work for the Pacman."

"The Pacman? You mean Lester Tree, Shady?"

I knew Shady. Hell, everyone knew him. He was a rare piece of work, into everything: protection, prostitution, porn, drugs, you name it. Everything short of murder, and I wouldn't put even that beyond him. I say *was* because I'd heard nothing about him for a while. I'd run into him several times before. I'd even shot him once, during an altercation. He used to operate out of a place off Bailey. The cops had been after him for years, but he'd never been arrested. So that was why I was having such a hard time with Benny. If anybody even mentioned Shady's name in the wrong place, they were likely to end up with their legs broken. That's why they call him the Pacman: he eats up his enemies, and the competition.

"Yeah, yeah, Shady Tree. That's all I know, damn it. Now get outa here an' leave me the hell alone, and stay outta my bar, you ugly bastard."

"Names, Benny. I need names. Who are they?"

"Come on, Harry. They'll hurt me if they find out I've been talking to you. Okay, okay. Put that damn gun away. The big guy, his name is Duvon James. The other, the small guy, is Henry Gold. They call 'em Gold and Silver. James is muscle; Gold is brains. You don't want to screw around with those two, I can tell ya. They'll bust your ass. Then again, maybe you should."

"What were they talking about?"

"I swear I don't know. You don't listen in on those two's talk. You just don't do it, an' I didn't, an' I don't—*ever!*"

I believed him. I got up off the desk, holstered the nine, and walked to the door.

"Keep your mouth shut, Benny. I was never here. You think Duvon and Henry are tough? Open your mouth and you'll find out how tough I can be. You hear me?"

He nodded.

"I'll see you tonight maybe."

And with that, I left him there, nursing his ear, tears running down his cheeks.

I returned to my car. I don't drive a fancy car. I could, but they attract too much attention. I drive a Nissan Maxima SL, midnight blue with all the bells and whistles, 300 horses and a Bose sound system that can make your teeth hurt. It's not your run-of-the-mill, off-the-shelf version either. I had a friend of mine tweak it a little. Now it can do zero to sixty in under five seconds. Comes in handy, sometimes.

I sat back and let the leather enfold me, pushed the button to start the motor, set the climate for seventy-two, and turned on the heated seat. I laid my head back, closed my eyes, and let my mind go over what Benny had told me.

What the hell was a girl like that doing with two of Shady's gangbangers? There's no way she's a hooker. Drugs maybe?

But I had no idea. I heaved a sigh, sat up, and punched up the Bluetooth. "Call Kate."

She picked up on the first ring. "What's up, Harry?"

"I'm on Broad. I had a talk with Benny."

"Benny at the Sorbonne? Did you get anything?"

"Oh yeah. Those two characters work for Lester Tree. Their names are Duvon James and Henry Gold."

"Never heard of 'em. Shady Tree, I do know. He's trouble, Harry, but he's been kinda quiet these past couple of years. Keeps a low profile. I'll see what I can find out. Anything else?"

"Not yet. I'm about to call Willard."

"'Okay. Later." She hung up.

I dialed Willard's number. It rang twice, and then he answered.

"Willard Residence."

"Dr. Willard?

"Speaking."

"Dr. Willard. This is Harry Starke. First, let me say that I'm sorry for your loss."

"Thank you, Mr. Starke. What can I do for you?" He didn't sound too upset.

"I think Lieutenant Gazzara mentioned that I'd like to talk to you about your daughter, Tabitha. I'd like to come on up, if that's convenient."

"I'm not sure I understand. Why do you want to talk to me about her? Aren't the police looking into her death?"

"No, sir. It was a suicide. I was there. On the bridge. I saw her jump." Silence.

"Are you still there, Doctor?"

More silence. I looked at the display on the dash. The timer was still running.

"Dr. Willard?"

"Yes, yes. Come on up. I'll be waiting."

"Twenty minutes."

"Fine."

Click.

He'd hung up.

4

The ride up Lookout Mountain was uneventful. No more than twenty minutes after my call to Dr. Willard, I turned onto the circular gravel drive in front of his home. Kate had been right. It was impressive, and yes, the garage was huge.

I parked the car in front of the house, walked up the five steps to the front door and rang the bell. He looked tired, wrung out, but he also looked as if he'd just stepped off the golf course: fancy slacks and a shirt that must have cost at least a couple of hundred bucks. I felt like I was under-dressed, and he must have thought I was, too, because he made no bones about eying me up and down.

"Mr. Starke?"

"Please. Call me Harry."

He nodded. "Come on in."

He took me into what I assumed must be his library. I'd never seen so many books in one place before. The room was huge and lined with shelves and looked even bigger due to the singular lack of furniture: jusr a huge partner's desk, a plush executive chair, a couple of leather easy chairs, and a matching sofa. The view from the big windows across the perfectly landscaped gardens was spectacular, even better than the view at my place. I could see up and down the Lookout Valley and then some.

"Take a seat, Mr. Starke. I already know who and what you are. I made some calls. You have quite a reputation. A good one, I might add. Now, talk to me. Tell me what happened last night."

I told him everything I'd seen. I told him about his daughter's presence in the Sorbonne and what had happened on the bridge. I told him everything, but I didn't tell him who the two bangers in the bar were or who they worked for. I needed to know more about them. Could be their meeting was innocent, but I didn't think so.

"So why are you here, Mr. Starke?"

I was silent for a moment, then I looked at him. "I'm not sure... I could tell she was scared out of her wits, but why? What could have frightened her so badly that she jumped off the bridge? We don't yet know if she had anything in her system, but I'm almost certain she wasn't high or drunk. I would have known if she was. She was frightened. *Really* frightened. I'd like to know why."

"Mr. Starke, Harry, I can't imagine why Tabitha would have done this. She was a very stable girl. Levelheaded. She isn't my only daughter. Her sister, Jessica, is eighteen months younger; she's twenty-three. They both live here. Well, only Jess now. There's an apartment over the garage, two of them, in fact. Anyway, I would also like to know what happened. I want you to look into it, officially. I want to hire you. Can I do that?"

"You can, but—"

"No. No buts. I need to do this, for her mother and her sister as much as for me." He opened one of the desk drawers and took out a checkbook and pen. "I know you need a retainer. How much would that be?"

"I charge two-fifty an hour plus expenses, which could be extensive. Time spent on the case by my operatives and secretarial work are charged separately. My retainer would be fifteen thousand."

He nodded, put pen to his checkbook, scribbled, then tore out the check and handed it to me.

"I made it for twenty-five. If you need more, let me know. I expect to be kept up to date with the investigation. I'd like you to call me every day. Can you do that?"

I shook my head. "No, sir. I can't promise to do that. That's not how I work. I'll communicate as needs be. I'll call you whenever I have something pertinent to tell you, or if I need answers to questions, but that's the only promise I can make."

He stared at me for a moment, then nodded.

"Good, then I'll have Jacque, my PA, draw up the paperwork and send it over for your signature. You should have it sometime tomorrow afternoon. Please get it back to her as soon as you can. I'll also need your cell phone number. Here's mine."

I handed him my card. He wrote his number on the back of one of his own and handed it to me.

"One more thing." I took my iPhone from my pocket and pulled up the photo of the pendant. "I know Lieutenant Gazzara showed you this pendant, but I want you to look at it again. Are you sure you've never seen it before? Your daughter was wearing it when they found her."

He took a look at the photo but shook his head.

"How about this key? Do you know what it's for?"

Again, he shook his head.

"All right then. Now, if you don't mind, I'd like to take a look at her rooms."

"Of course. I'll take you."

It was quite a hike: out of the rear door onto a patio, past an enormous pool complex and across the courtyard. The apartments were side by side over the garage. Tabitha's was closest to the main house.

The door to the stairs was unlocked; the door to the apartment was not. Willard took a bunch of keys from his pocket, slid one into the lock, turned it, pushed the door open then he stepped aside for me to enter.

I crossed the threshold and stopped just inside. I wanted to get an over-all view of the room—first impressions are important.

It wasn't as opulent as I thought it would be. Oh, it was quite special, but I had the feeling that Tabitha hadn't spent much time there. The furniture was expensive, and so were the window treatments and carpet, as you might expect. The apartment included four rooms: a large living room comfortable, elegant, and furnished throughout by Williams-Sonoma.

Not a stick out of place.

The small kitchenette, as far as I could tell, was unused. The bedroom also had a feeling of vacancy about it. Unconsciously, I shrugged my shoulders, and then I noticed that Willard was staring at me, questioningly.

"Was Tabitha married, Doctor Willard?"

He smiled. "She *was* married. It was a long time ago, when she was nineteen. It didn't last long, thank God...."

It was then that I think it hit him: she was gone, for good.

He seemed to deflate. He pushed past me and sat down on one of the bedroom chairs. He gulped, shook his head, and then seemed to regain some of his composure, but it was still there: his eyes were watering.

I left him alone, sitting there, staring at the bed. I stepped into the bathroom. *Oh boy, ladies do love their bathrooms.* The rest of the apartment might not have been luxurious, but the bathroom certainly was. It wouldn't have been out of place in Buckingham Palace. I looked into one of the mirrors and spotted Willard standing in the doorway.

"I get the feeling she didn't spend much time here," I said.

He nodded. "Well, not as often as she once did. I think she came here when she needed time to herself, weekends mostly, to get away from the city. She stayed with a friend, downtown. Easier than traveling up and down the mountain, so she said."

"Friend? What friend?"

"Charlotte... Charlie Maxwell."

I nodded. Kate had mentioned her.

"They'd been friends almost all their lives. They were in high school together, Baylor, and then they were in college together, Princeton.... Charlie doesn't know about Tab. I need to call her." He turned and walked back into the living room.

"One moment, please, Dr. Willard."

He stopped, half turned, and looked at me.

"She already knows. Lieutenant Gazzara has already talked to her."

He nodded absently.

"Do you have a photo of Tabitha I can borrow? I'll make sure it's returned as soon as possible."

He walked to the dresser, picked up two frames and handed them to me. One had a close-up of two girls, both in their mid-twenties; both were smiling, happy. I recognized the redhead on the left as Tabitha Willard.

"This must be Charlie." I pointed to the second girl.

He nodded.

The other photo was a broader shot of three girls sitting together on a sofa. Tabitha and Charlie, and another girl. I held it up for him to see.

"Jess.... That's Jessica, our other daughter. She has the other apartment, next to this one."

"Did Tabitha have a boyfriend, anyone serious?"

He nodded. "I don't know much about him, just his first name, Michael. I don't think she's been seeing him lately, though. She never brought him home. That is to say, I never saw them here. I've certainly never met him."

I made a mental note of the name. "Could you tell me a little about Jessica?"

He nodded absently. "She looks a lot like Tab but colors her hair blond. She's twenty-three years old, she'll graduate UTC next year. Psychology. She has a boyfriend named Will Dyson. He's a bit older than I care for, twenty-eight, but seems like a nice kid, what we've seen of him. She comes and goes as she pleases.... We don't see as much of her as we'd like either, but... well, children are children, very independent at that age."

I was beginning to worry about him. He looked as if he was about to fall asleep.

"I'll take another quick look around, if you don't mind."

He nodded, and then let his chin drop, almost onto his chest.

I took out a small digital recorder and began a tour of the

apartment, recording my thoughts and taking pictures with my iPhone. It was, I was sure, a waste of time. Nothing untoward caught my attention, but I was able to get a feel for the girl. She was high maintenance. I was sure of that. Her closets—there were two of them—were filled with expensive clothes. There must have been sixty or seventy pairs of shoes, all expensive.

No jewelry. Hmmm. Must have left it at her friend Charlie's place.

Her drawers were filled with expensive lingerie, not overly provocative, but, well, you know, expensive. Not the kind of stuff you'd find at JCPenny. The bathroom vanity showed little personality. Kate's bathroom was always a mess; this one was not. There were several bottles of expensive perfume on the vanity. I picked up one of the bottles, turned it over in my hand.

Body Milk. What the hell is that?

There was also a bottle of Coco Chanel's Coco Mademoiselle. None of it was the kind of stuff a girl would wear every day at the office. *Then again, maybe they would. What the hell do I know?* Other than the perfume and a few odds and ends of makeup, there were no other personal items present. I opened a drawer: face cloths. I opened another: a hair dryer. I opened one of the cupboards: towels.

"When was the last time she was here, Doctor?"

He thought for a moment. "A week ago last Sunday, I think. I'm not entirely sure. I can check with my wife, if you like."

"If you wouldn't mind, sir. There's no need to do it now. You can give me a call later today."

But he already had his phone in his hand and was

punching in the number. He didn't say much, just asked the question and then hung up.

"Sunday, ten days ago. Is it important?"

"Probably not. I'm just trying to tie up loose ends. What did Tabitha do for a living?"

"She worked in public relations, some company out of New York. She didn't need to. I gave her an allowance. With that, and what she earned at her job, she was never short of money."

"An allowance?"

He nodded. "Yes. Not a big one. Fifteen hundred a week. If she needed anything... a car, things like that, I helped her with that, too. She knew she could always come to me, for anything, but she rarely ever did. She was a good girl, never any trouble at all, Tabitha."

"Dr. Willard, you said her allowance was six thousand a month, and that she was working in public relations, for a company out of New York."

"Yes, that's correct."

"She was wearing a coat last night that must have cost more than four thousand; her closets are filled with very expensive clothes and shoes, at least another hundred thousand dollars worth. Her income was not enough to support such expenditures. Do you have any idea where the money came from?"

He looked at me, bewildered, and shook his head.

"Well, never mind. It's something for me to look into... Doctor Willard, I'll take up no more of your time today, but I may need to talk to you again soon. In any case, I'll keep you updated about any progress I make, but it's going to take a while. Please try to be patient."

He rose stiffly to his feet, looking for all the world like a whipped dog. I couldn't help but feel sorry for him.

He followed me down the stairs and out onto the courtyard. He reached out to me with both hands, one for my hand, the other for my shoulder.

"Please, Mr. Starke. Her mother and I need to know. She wasn't a bad girl, and we loved her dearly."

What could I say to that? Not much. So I didn't say anything. I simply squeezed his hand gently, nodded, then got into my car and drove away. I could see him in the rearview mirror, watching me.

How the hell does anyone cope with losing a daughter? I had no answer to that question. I felt sorry for the man. *Well, I'll do my best.*

Jessica Willard was a younger version of her sister. She didn't want to talk, but it had to be done. Unfortunately, there was nothing for her to tell me. She was close to her sister, but they lived very different lives and saw each other only when they ran into one another, either in town or when they were at home together.

Jessica knew about Michael, but she didn't know they'd split up, and she seemed quite surprised to hear it. She was under the impression that he was very fond of Tabitha, and she him. No, she didn't know his last name. No, she hadn't seen her in more than a week.

She didn't know any more than her father had, and she was grieving, so I thanked her, said goodbye, and left her to it.

5

I hadn't been home more than thirty minutes when my cell phone rang. It was Kate.

"Hey, it's me. I need to see you."

I looked at my watch. It was almost eight o'clock. "What? Right now? I just got in. I need to take a shower."

"It's important."

"What's so important it can't wait until morning?"

"I can't say over the phone."

"Cut it out, Kate. I'm tired and in no mood for riddles. What do you want?"

"I'll tell you when you get here. Get your ass over here."

"Kate, it's... Oh geez. Where's here?"

"My place, dummy. Where do you think?"

I heaved a sigh. "Well, I thought you might be at work. Okay, gimme a half hour, maybe forty-five minutes. Make some coffee."

"You got it."

I didn't bother to shower. I splashed cold water on my

face, ran my wet fingers through my hair, brushed my teeth, and headed out the door. *What the hell can be so important?*

Kate has an apartment at Forest Cove in East Brainerd, ten miles away from where I live. I was there in twenty minutes.

The imposing hump of Lookout Mountain was a black silhouette studded with diamonds against the night sky, the lights of the homes of the rich and... well, you get the idea. The sky itself was a vast star field, Orion and the Seven Sisters high overhead. Beautiful. I thumbed the bell. The door opened almost immediately.

She was wearing a T-shirt, one of mine, that went all the way down to her knees. Her hair was down. She wore no makeup. This was the real Kate Gazzara.

"Come in, Harry." She stepped aside to let me pass, and then closed the door behind me, flipped the two locks, and followed me into her kitchen.

"I thought you had a hot date."

"No date, Harry. I was just kidding. Briefing. Which is why I need to see you. Sit down."

I sat down at the small breakfast table and watched as she poured two cups of coffee, both black, handed one to me, and set the other one down on the table opposite. I said nothing. Waited. She looked worried. Obviously, she had something on her mind. I sipped my coffee, let her think about it.

She went to the window, stood with her back to me, staring out. She turned, walked to the table, sat down, and picked up her cup.

"Harry, what I'm about to tell you must not leave this room. If it gets out, I'll lose my job. You promise?"

I nodded. "You know me better than that, Kate."

"Yeah, I know you all right, better than I probably should."

I wasn't quite sure how to take that.

"We're opposites, Kate, you and me, and that's a good thing. We work well together. What I don't see, you usually do, and vice versa. I trust you. I think you trust me. You can do things, go places, and talk to people that I can't. You're a cop; I used to be. I don't have to answer or report to anyone. That's why we make a good team."

I stared at her across the table. She had her head down, looking at her cup, which she was holding in both hands. Her face was pale.

"Kate. How long has it been? Sixteen years? You know you can trust me with your life. I sure as hell trust you with mine. So tell me."

"What do you know about Gordon Harper?"

I thought for a moment. The name was familiar, but.... Then the light went on. "You mean Little Billy Harper? Congressman Gordon Harper?"

"Yes. He hates that name. Apparently, it was something his grandfather laid on him when he was a baby. 'Little Billy,' after himself. The old man, Granddad Billy, was Representative William George Harper, one-time Speaker of the Tennessee House. He was... well... less than honest? No, he was a bad one, the old man. Greasy as they come, but nothing ever stuck to him. Some people think Little Billy is a chip off the old block. The old man retired in 1990 and died a year later."

I nodded. I'd heard of the late Billy Harper, but what Kate was saying was new to me. But then, he'd been dead twenty-five years. I was still in high school when Big Billy was playing his games.

"So what's with the congressman then?"

"He announced his candidacy for the U.S. Senate a couple of days ago. Hell, Harry, don't you ever watch the news?"

I grinned. "Not if I can help it. So what if he's running for the senate? He'll never unseat old man Jennings."

"There's the rub, Harry. He has more than enough money to buy the seat, and no one can figure out where it's coming from. He's dirty. He'll do what it takes. He has a lot of important people in his pocket."

"Wait, how do you know he's dirty? He's sure as hell popular. Wasn't he responsible for pushing the Senior Aid Bill through Congress, after the Republicans deflated Medicaid?"

"I don't know for sure that he is dirty; it's more a gut feeling than anything else. The Senior Aid Bill brought him a lot of good will and some hefty donations, but apparently it wasn't enough. Now he's pushing an Immigration/Homeland Security agenda, also very popular. And he's raising and spending a lot of money, most of it under the table, maybe even laundering it through the Harper Foundation, so they think."

"They? Who's they?"

"You figure it out, Harry."

"Why are the Feds looking at Harper all of a sudden?"

"Not all of a sudden. They always have been. Started with the old man, but they couldn't make anything stick. They took an interest in Gordon the minute he got himself elected to Congress. They still have nothing on him, but they want to, and they think he's up to something, but they don't know what.

"I'm thinking the money, at least some of it, is coming

from the Billy Harper Foundation. That's a huge pot of gold, almost half a billion dollars, so I'm told. It's hard to believe that Little Billy could keep his sticky fingers out of it."

"But that's strictly regulated, surely."

"So it might be, but where there's a will there's a way, and I know damn well that Harper has the will, and he's done it before. At least we think he has."

"Okay, I get it, but what does all this have to do with Tabitha Willard? And why are you telling me about it?"

"It probably has nothing to do with her, but maybe.... Harry, I've been asking around. There's word on the street that Lester Tree is in Harper's pocket. Exactly how, we don't know. That's where you come in."

"That's where I come in? How do you figure?"

"I can't go after Harper, or Tree, or the Harper Foundation, not with the Feds being involved, but you can."

"You think? Okay, I could, but why would I?"

"Tabitha Willard, for one. Our two heroes, James and Gold, work for Tree, who works for Harper, maybe. It makes sense, right?"

I nodded. It did make sense, and I owed Tree one, too. "I'll think about it."

"The girl. Why'd she jump, Harry?"

"I've been thinking about that. I talked to her father earlier today. Nothing. She was frightened, Kate. I mean she was really scared, but that was no reason to do what she did. She wasn't being chased. Maybe she thought she was. Maybe she knew or saw something she shouldn't. But I was there, and I know she wasn't being chased. So, that only leaves me, right?"

I paused for a moment, looked her in the eye. "Kate. I think she jumped because of me. I think she thought I was one of them, waiting for her. Maybe if I hadn't been there she would still be alive. I feel really bad about it, and *that's* reason enough for me to get involved."

"You can't think like that, Harry. It wasn't your fault."

"Maybe not, but I can't get her face out of my mind. You should have seen the look, Kate. She was petrified. I'll get to the bottom of it, though. And when I do...."

"Harry." She looked hard at me. "You'll be discreet, right? Harper has some very powerful friends."

"So do I."

She sighed and shook her head. "What about Dr. Willard? How did that go?"

"Well, he hired me. So now I have a legitimate reason to look into her death. The interview.... It went okay, about what you'd expect. I need some time to sift through it, but nothing obvious jumped out at me. She was married once, for a short time, way back when, and she had a sister, some friends. You already met Charlotte Maxwell; she was her best friend. I'll need to talk to her. There was also a boyfriend, although Willard seemed to think that ended several weeks ago. Michael something. He didn't know the last name. I need to find out what it is. Talk to him."

"So, there you are then. She gets dumped, she's depressed, gets drunk, and decides to end it all."

"I don't think so, for several reasons, the most important being that if I hadn't been on that bridge, I don't think she would have jumped. Hell, Kate, the girl had everything to live for. She was beautiful... damn."

She looked at me for a while, sort of sadly, then looked up at the kitchen clock. "It's late, Harry. Time for you to go."

I looked at her, eyebrows raised.

She smiled, shook her head. "No, Harry. Not tonight. I have to go in early tomorrow."

I smiled at her, got up from the table, and walked to the door. She followed me. I opened the door, turned to say goodnight. She was close. She leaned in, grasped both of my arms at the elbows, and kissed me gently on the lips. "Goodnight, Harry. Call me tomorrow, 'kay?"

She closed the door softly behind me.

6

I slept like the dead that night. I didn't wake until almost seven thirty, which was late for me. I'm normally in the office by then. I shoved my mug under the coffee maker and hit the button, then took a quick shower. I threw on my usual black slacks, white tee, and leather jacket, slipped into my loafers, grabbed the coffee, and ran down the stairs and out into the garage. I was in the office by eight twenty. Jacque was waiting for me—wasn't she always?

Now Jacque Hale, my personal assistant, is a very special kid. I say kid. She's twenty-seven years old, has a Masters degree in business administration and a bachelor's in criminology: quite a combination, which is one of the reasons I hired her even before she got out of college. I liked the kid. She's attractive; when she smiles, she lights up the room. She's a little on the skinny side, tall, with long black hair. She has a great sense of humor and a wonderful personality, but she can be serious when she needs to be, especially when she's around me and in the office. Her parents are Jamaican. I love them both dearly.

I walked into the outer office through the side door. She looked at me, the accusation unspoken.

"I'm late," I said. "So what?"

"I've been waitin' for you. There are messages. There are papers for you to look over and sign, and I know you: a quick cup of coffee and you'll be out of here."

"Let's go." I grinned at her back as she pushed open the door to my office and marched inside. She was right. There were a half-dozen messages and a sheaf of papers half an inch thick. Fortunately, it wasn't as bad as it looked. Many of the papers had been sorted into groups and stapled.

"Judge Sharpe called," she said. "Can you call him back this afternoon, after five? He's in court all day."

"I can do that."

"I'll remind you."

I grinned at her. She did not smile back.

"Also, Larry Soames called. He didn't say what he wanted, and I *did* ask him. He said he would tell you himself." I could tell she wasn't too pleased about that.

"Soames?"

She nodded. "He probably wants to hire you."

"Hah. Well, we'll see. I'll call him later."

"I'll remind you of that, too."

There were a couple more messages, but nothing important. I told her I'd make the calls before I left, and I waited. She just looked at me, her eyebrows raised in question.

"Nothing from Kate?" I asked.

"No!"

I've always had the impression that Jacque doesn't altogether approve of my relationship with Kate. Something about conflict of interest. I heard her murmur it one day as she walked out of my office.

"So," she said, "what are your plans for today?"

"How's my schedule look? I have a couple of things I need to do, and they're kind of urgent."

"Well, *after* you make your calls, you have a couple of client appointments this afternoon, nothing I can't reschedule, but I can only do it once. When would you like to see them?"

Now when Jacque makes a promise on my behalf, I know I have to keep it. If I don't, she takes it personally, so I knew I needed to be careful. I thought for a moment, and then said, "How about Friday morning?"

She flipped the pages on my desk calendar. "A quarter after eight, and nine thirty. Good?"

I nodded. I hate making appointments for Fridays. Oh well. I looked at my watch. It was nine o'clock. I got up from my desk to grab a second cup of coffee, then sat down again to think. *Shady Tree. Hmmm. Why were your boys arguing with Tabitha? Time to find out, I think.*

I swallowed the rest of my coffee, then breezed out through the office.

"Later, Jacque, later," I said as she started to rise from her seat. "Call if you need me, okay?"

7

I knew where to find Shady Tree—or at least I thought I did. It was nearly ten o'clock when I pulled up outside the rundown, two-story tenement building just off Bailey—four one-time town homes that had seen their best days more than fifty years ago. Each home, a term that stretched the bounds of reality, had a flight of six steps from the sidewalk to the front door. On either side of the steps, each unit had a low wall with concrete toppers. Back in the last century when they were built, there might have been ornamental iron railings set atop them, but not now. Seated on the walls were five men, rough-looking types varying in age from maybe seventeen to thirty.

I got out of the car, made a point of locking the door, and walked toward them. They were typical of the brand. One on one, they were nothing. As a group, they were probably killers.

As I approached, they straightened themselves and tried to look tough. I picked out the one I assumed to be the leader, a scruffy, heavy-set dude with a beard, dreads, and one of those big rainbow tams on his head.

"Hey, you," I said to him.

He stared sullenly back at me.

"Go tell Mr. Tree that Harry Starke's here to see him."

He stood up. He was at least six feet tall. The other four also stood; they had his back, I presumed.

"Wha' foh you wan' 'im?"

"None of your damn business. Now go tell him."

He put his right hand behind his back and took a step forward. I brought my right hand up inside my open jacket and let him see the M&P9, my hand resting on the grip. He stopped, nodded, then took a step back.

"He ain' here."

"Okay. So where is he?"

"He wanna see you?"

"He does. He will."

He nodded, sat down again. The other four followed suit.

"He over on McCallie. Strip mall near duh ol' church. He own it. Cain' miss it."

I knew where he was talking about, but I didn't recall a strip mall.

I pushed the button on the keyless fob, unlocked the car door, and stepped backward, my hand still resting on the nine. I never once took my eyes off the big guy until I was in the car with the door closed behind me. I could see them in the rearview mirror, watching as I drove away.

No wonder I didn't know the strip mall. It was brand new, an upscale, two-story strip with six nice-looking ground floor stores, including one at the north end that had tinted windows. Someone had covered the inside of the glass with some sort of dark, opaque film, probably the same stuff they use to tint car windows. I grinned. This, I was sure, was where I would find Shady.

I parked the Maxima out front and walked the few yards to the front door. It was locked. In fact, there wasn't even a handle, just a bell push. I pushed. I waited. I pushed again. An eye appeared at a small round hole in the film. I signaled with a finger for the eye to open the door, and it did, just a crack.

"We don' wan' none."

I rammed my shoulder against the stainless-steel doorframe, taking the eye by surprise. As the door flew open, I heard him stagger a couple of steps back. I pushed the door open. He'd tripped and landed on his ass. He was short, and way overweight, with a big red welt across his forehead where the door had hit him. A small-caliber semi-automatic stuck out of his waistband.

"Don't even think about it," I said, showing him my own.

"Wha' fo' you do dat? Wadda hell you want?" he yelled as he struggled to his feet.

"I want to see Shady, and I want to see him *now*!"

He jumped at the shout. "Okay, okay. I'll tell him. Who you is?"

"Tell him Harry Starke is here to see him."

He backed up a half-dozen steps along the short passageway, keeping his eye on me and his hand on the gun. Without looking away, he put out his left hand and pushed open a door.

"They's a Harry Starke here, Mr. Tree. Says he wanna see you."

"*Harry Starke*? You gotta be kiddin' me. You got balls, I'll say that for you." The shout was followed out into the passage by the man himself. He was grinning broadly, but I wasn't fooled for a second.

"Come on in." He waved me through into his office. And there they were, Duvon James and Henry Gold.

The big guy, Duvon, was wearing the same quilted jacket he'd had on at the Sorbonne—and sunglasses. Gold, however, had stepped it up a notch. He looked like he'd just stepped out of a 1940s movie: double-breasted pin-striped suit, white shirt, black slim-Jim tie, and a do rag, for God's sake. I couldn't help myself. I looked at him and shook my head. I could see by the look on his face that he didn't like it, not one bit.

"Take a seat, Mr. Starke."

Mr. Starke? Geez.

Tree motioned to one of two chairs in front of the desk. They were both too low. The legs had been shortened, and neither one looked strong enough to hold the small guy, Gold, let alone me. I wasn't about give him that kind of advantage. I grabbed one from the side of the room instead and sat down in front of a desk that would have made a banker envious.

"What might I do for you, Mr. Starke?" Tree asked, as he lowered himself gently down into an executive chair that must have cost almost as much as my Maxima. I could hear the air whistle out of the over-stuffed upholstery as he sank into it. *Maybe it wasn't air at all.*

This was a different Shady Tree than the one I was familiar with. He was smooth, a changed man. Not the street jock with the do rag he'd been the last time I saw him. No Ebonics, no street slang. The accent was almost refined, but not quite. He wore a nice, conservative gray suit, a pale blue shirt, and a maroon tie. Even the dreads were neat and shiny clean.

"Wow, Shady. You've come up in the world. You win the lottery or rob a bank?"

"Neither one, my friend. I am just a businessman, doing well."

"Businessman, my ass. You're a crook, Shady. You always were. You always will be. You can't help yourself. You're into everything. Hookers, drugs, guns, protection, you name it. And," I nodded toward Duvon and Gold, "businessmen don't need creeps like those two to guard their backs. Oh, and I'm not your friend."

Duvon took a step forward. Gold didn't move. Tree held up his hand. Duvon stopped.

I looked across the desk at Tree. "Keep your dog on a tight leash, Shady. He steps into my space, I'll geld him."

Duvon growled something I couldn't understand, but he stepped back, his hands clasped together in front of his jeans, as if he was covering his package. Whether it was what I'd said about gelding him, or just a comfortable way for him to stand, I had no idea, but I grinned up at him anyway. The look on his face was priceless. I held his gaze for a moment, then turned my attention to Gold.

Where the hell did Tree find these two? We have some pretty tough characters in Chattanooga, but these two? *Big city boys? New York, maybe? D.C.?*

Duvon was an easy read. He was a tough soldier who provided the muscle Tree must need on a daily basis. They come a dime a dozen, his sort. The street gangs breed them by the thousands. Gold, however, was a totally different type. He was indeed a small man, no more than five seven and slim. No, skinny. He was probably anorexic. That stupid suit was at least a size too big for him. But as ridiculous as he looked in his outfit, he had an air about him. *This one is dangerous.* His hair was dyed jet black; his narrow face was dominated by a sharp beak of a nose that looked too big for his face; his eyes were narrow slits of hate; his mouth was slightly parted in an icy half-smile. It was a look a shark would have been proud of. This was one to watch, carefully, a psychopath if ever I saw one.

"Hey, Starke. You awake?"

I came out of my reverie and smiled.

"I tell you, Starke. I run a legitimate business now. I have my rentals over on Bailey that bring in a nice piece of change, and I have this sweet little mall. I own all the businesses in it. Ladies' clothing, men's clothing, the gym, cigar store, the restaurant. Don't believe me? Check 'em out. They're all above board, and legal."

"Shady, I need your help."

He looked at me as if he was talking to a half-wit. Then he burst into laugher. "That'll be the day, Starke. You got a hell of a lot of nerve. You come in here, shovin' your weight around, and then you ask for my help. You're one crazy son of a bitch, an' I ain't forgotten this, either." He pulled up his left sleeve and showed me the dimpled scar on his wrist. The result of a bullet I'd pumped into him a couple of years ago when I was working the Robinson case.

"One of these days you gonna pay for d'pain an' rehab I had ta go tru after you clipped my ass. I was outta work more'n two mont's."

I smiled. The accent had slipped a couple of notches.

"Shady, you never did a real day's work in your life. Now tell me what you know about Tabitha Willard."

Out of the corner of my eye, I saw Duvon's mouth twitch when I said her name.

"Who? Tabitha who?"

"Oh come on, Shady. You know who. I saw your boys, Stimpy and Ren there," I nodded at the dynamic duo behind him, "arguing with her Monday night in the Sorbonne."

They didn't like that at all, being called Stimpy and Ren.

"The classy white bitch?" Gold said. "We wuz jus' tryin' to pick 'er up. Get us some o' dat fine white ass."

"Bullshit. You were arguing. All three of you. Thirty minutes later she came running out of the Sorbonne like the devil was on her tail. What did you do or say to scare her so bad she threw herself off the Walnut Street Bridge?"

Duvon looked at me with wide eyes. Gold was slowly shaking his head. What I'd said was news to both of them. They obviously didn't know she was dead.

"Nothin'. We din't do nothing," Gold said slowly. "Like I said, we was jus' tryin' to pick 'er up, man. She fine. Tol' Duvon to go screw 'imsef. Bitch!"

"I was in that bar on Monday night. I saw what happened. You were arguing with the woman, not trying to pick her up. A half hour later, I was on the bridge when she came running toward me, scared stiff. She took one look at me, probably thought I was one of you assholes, and then she took a header over the rail into the water. The fall killed her."

I watched all three of them. Gold's left eye twitched. Duvon clasped his package a little tighter. Shady smiled that nasty little smile I knew so well, only this time he showed teeth so white they almost twinkled.

"Now I feel really bad that it was me who caused her to jump, and I don't like that, Shady. And I'm going to find out why she jumped, what frightened her so much that she figured it would be better to die than to face whatever it was. I think you know what that was, Shady. In fact, I know you know."

I thought for a moment, and then decided to play the Hail Mary.

I looked across the desk. "Okay. For now, let's say I buy into the story that these two clowns were hitting on her." I rolled my eyes at them. "So let's talk about something else. What about Little Billy Harper, Shady? What's your connection to him?"

Now that did get a reaction. Tree leaned back in his chair, his eyes narrowed almost to slits. He rested his elbows on the arms of the chair and steepled his fingers, cocked his head to one side, and smiled. If a barracuda could smile, it would look just like Shady did then.

"Little Billy who? I don't know anyone by that name. In fact, I have no idea what you're talking about, Starke." It was said almost in a whisper, so quietly I could barely hear him. The refined accent had returned, with a vengeance.

I decided not to push it. I didn't need to. His reaction had told me what I wanted to know, and I was sure he would pass the message on, which was what I wanted anyway. I'd made my play. I'd thrown a little chum onto the waters. It would spread. Fish would bite. Now all I had to do was wait and be ready to snag one.

I sat there for a long moment, staring at him, waiting for him to break. He didn't. The steely eyes never blinked.

"Nothing to say, Shady?"

He didn't answer, just sat there, rocking gently back and forth, the springs in the chair squeaking in time with the motion of the chair. I got to my feet, opened my jacket, and let my hand rest on the grip of the M&P9. I backed up to the door, pulled it open and paused, all the time never taking my eyes off him, or his two clippers.

"I'll be back, Shady. Bet on it."

Hah, what's that saying? If looks could kill?

I stepped quickly out into the hallway and pulled the door shut behind me.

When I got back out into the open—the air outside was a lot fresher, but cold—I decided to do as Shady had suggested and check out the businesses in his mall. I stepped back, all the way to the curb. For a strip mall, it was very fancy, faux Spanish architecture that was out of place in this part of town. Hell, it was out of place anywhere in town, a two-story affair that must have cost at least twenty million to build.

Aside from Shady's unit there was Angelique, an upscale store selling ladies apparel, Chester Knight, an equally upscale men's clothing store, The Gym, which speaks for itself, Le Fume, a high price smoke shop selling expensive cigars and French cigarettes, and finally La Maison Ducat, an upscale French restaurant. What there might be on the upper floor, who knew.

With the exception of the restaurant, they were all open for business. The two clothing stores were quiet, just a couple of customers in each, but they were certainly shopping. The smoke shop wasn't very busy either. It could have been a jeweler's store, but instead of diamonds and watches, the glass cases were humidors filled with expensive smokes. It almost made me want to start smoking again. The gym was a different story. It was a hive of activity. Dozens of sweaty bodies worked expensive machines, and there had to be least ten exotic-looking personal trainers, male and female.

Maybe Kate can check it out for me.

The restaurant was even more special. I looked through glass windows into a quiet world of linen-covered tables, crystal glasses, and polished silver flatware. A discreet sign inside the door informed me that La Maison Ducat was open Tuesday through Saturday, from six o'clock in the evening. The closing time wasn't listed. I would have to take Kate for a night out and give it a try. I might even try the gym myself. I walked around the block. The back was almost as nice as the front. A balcony ran the full length of the rear of the building. Each unit was separated by a privacy wall. There was enough parking for at least a hundred cars.

So, Shady isn't lying. These were all legitimate businesses. Except for his unit, of course. But I wasn't buying it. I knew Shady well, and restaurants were not his bag, let alone the high-class boutiques. It all had to be a front, but for what? I had no idea.

I looked at my watch. It was getting on toward noon. I took out my phone and dialed Kate's number.

"Hey, Harry. What's up?"

"You want some lunch?"

"Sure. Where? When?"

"Cheddars, on Gunbarrel Road. Twenty minutes."

"Okay. See you there."

A minute later, I was in the Maxima and heading north. It had been an interesting thirty minutes.

8

W*ow. This lady's a cop?* Kate was already there when I arrived, standing just outside the front entrance door. *My God, she's lovely.* She was wearing a black business suit with a skirt that ended maybe two inches above the knee, a white, scoop-neck tee under the jacket, and three-inch heels. Understated, but stunning.

"Good God, Harry." She looked me up and down. "You look like a thug."

"You don't look so bad yourself." I grinned at her, leaned in, pecked her on the cheek, took her elbow, and escorted her inside.

Okay, you got it. By now, you've probably figured it out: the relationship between us was a little more than professional.

We go back a long way, Kate and me. I've known her since she was twenty-two, a rookie cop. And.... Well, we've been an item of sorts almost ever since. I think the world of her, and she knows it. I've been trying to recruit her for years, but she won't have it; something about "too much of a good thing."

I pulled Kate's seat out for her to sit down, and I sat opposite her. We made small talk until the waiter arrived.

Kate ordered a chicken Caesar salad and a Coke; I ordered a Philly cheesesteak and a Blue Moon beer, no orange slice.

As soon as the food came, Kate was all business. "So how did it go?"

"I had fun." I took a bite of my sandwich and chewed slowly, watched her eyes.

"Well?"

"Well what?"

"Oh come on, Harry. Don't tease. How did it go with Shady?"

I leaned forward and took a sip of beer. "It's complicated. I don't quite know what to make of him. He's certainly come up in the world. Says he's a businessman, a man of property." I paused for a moment, pulled out my phone and made a note that I needed to check that out, have someone take a look at the property records. See whose name was on the deeds.

"Property? What property? The only property Tree owns that I know of is that block of rancid rentals he owns on Bailey, and he's owned those for as long as I can remember."

"So he does, but have you seen that new strip mall up on McCallie, not far from the old church?"

She nodded, then said, "No way. I've shopped there. In fact, that's where I got this suit. That strip must have cost at least ten million. Where would he get that kind of money? He sure as hell couldn't get a mortgage."

"More like twenty," I said, "and it's out of place where it

is. That area just doesn't rate a strip of high-end businesses like those. That restaurant is something else. We should give it a try. My treat. What do you say?" I grinned at her.

"Sure, why not. Maybe we'll learn something."

"Right. I'll figure it out. You care which evening?"

"Nope. Whatever works for you."

I nodded. "You know, there's no telling where he got the money, but I aim to find out. He made no bones about the fact that he owned the strip."

"What about Tabitha? Any connection?"

"Oh, we talked about her at length. Those two gutter rats were there, and they know something, of that I'm sure. Gold said they were trying to pick her up, but I don't buy it. I can't figure why she'd be in the Sorbonne. She was a class act, and that place is dangerous. I've never seen her in there before."

"Maybe she was just slumming, looking for a bit of rough."

"Nah, I don't think so. Rough is one thing. Risking a dose of something nasty, something you're not likely to get rid of easily, is something else again. And anyway, her body language was all wrong. I'm sure she was arguing with them, and why did she run? And what in God's name could have scared her so much she took a header off the bridge?"

We ate in silence for several minutes, both of us deep in thought.

"And Harper?" she asked finally. "What about him? Any connection to Tree?"

"That's a tough one. I threw Tree a bone. I got a reaction, but he denied knowing him. I figure if there is a connection, he'll call Harper. If so, I'll know it when I get to see him. Harper, that is. If I get to see him."

"You'll figure it out. You always do." She put her hand in

her jacket pocket and fished out the pendant. "Any thoughts about this?" She handed it to me.

I held it by its edges, so that we both could see it. "No, I showed the photo of it to Willard. I thought as he'd had some time to think, he might have remembered, but no. Do you think it's significant?"

She slowly shook her head. "I don't know. Probably not. Maybe. Hang onto it. Show it around if you like. It's not doing either of us any good in my pocket."

"It's evidence. How..."

"Evidence of what?" she replied. "She committed suicide. You can return it to the family when you're done with it."

I nodded, held it in the palm of my hand. The serpents seemed to have a life of their own. I tossed it a few inches into the air. It twinkled under the artificial lights, flashing red and gold. I caught it and slipped it into the inside pocket of my jacket.

"I still need to talk to the friend, Charlotte Maxwell. They seemed close. Maybe she can shed some light on the story. We'll see."

"When will you see Harper?"

"The sooner the better. Maybe tomorrow morning."

"Discreet, Harry. Be discreet."

"Oh, I will. Don't worry. I'll have Jacque call him and make an appointment."

"How will you pull that off? He's a congressman; you don't just walk into his office."

I thought for a moment. She was right. I had to have a reason. Even I can't just walk in on one of the South's most prominent politicians.

"Dunno. I'll think of something... maybe dear old Dad can help."

"Hah, good old Dad. When are you going to cut the string, Harry?"

"I'm not. Why would I? He's my secret weapon, my best asset. Anyway, you like him, and he sure as hell loves you."

She nodded. "I love him, too. Pity he's not twenty-five years younger. I'd trade you for him in a heartbeat."

"You couldn't handle him."

"Oh, and why the hell not?"

I grinned at her and looked at my watch. It was just after one thirty. Time to go back to work.

"Time I wasn't here, Kate."

We made arrangements to meet later that evening—I'd cook dinner—said our goodbyes, and went our separate ways, Kate back to the Department, me to the office.

The first thing I did when I got back to the office was call my father. Fortunately, he wasn't in court, and his secretary put me straight through.

"Hey, Dad. It's me."

"Hey, son. How's it going?"

"Great, but I need a favor. I need to visit Congressman Harper, and I need an excuse. I need to use you. Or at least your name."

"Um... okay. You want to tell me about it?"

"There's not much to tell. Kate seems to think he's up to something; she has an idea that he's bilking the family foundation, money laundering, maybe. There's talk that he might be siphoning cash out of the foundation for his campaign. But who knows? I also have a feeling he may be connected to some very nasty operators. Anyway, she asked me to take a look."

"Be careful, Harry. Be very careful. Hell, he could be our next senator."

"Yeah, but I promised Kate, and I can't just walk in on him without a reason. And... well, there's something else. I'm looking into Tabitha Willard's death. There's a chance he might be involved in that, too, though for the life of me I can't see how."

"I thought she committed suicide... Harry, you saw her do it. What's to investigate?"

"I'm not sure, but the word is that Lester Tree works for Harper—and I *know* Tree had something to do with it."

Silence. Then: "I suppose I could make a donation to the foundation. You could take a check. But why would I? Harper's no fool. I'd need a reason, and a good one."

"How about a campaign donation?"

"Better. Consider it done. I'll send a check for $2,700 to your office. That's the max allowable under Federal law. You'll have it by four o'clock."

"What do you want me to tell him? What's the reason for the donation?"

"Come on, Harry. You can handle that, for God's sake. Tell him I like what he did with the Senior Aid Bill. Whatever you like. If he wants to call me, you can tell him he can. How's that?"

"Perfect. Thanks."

"Let me know how it goes."

Click.

That was Dad for you. No goodbye, no see you later.

Four o'clock. That meant I had some time to kill. I picked

up the office phone and buzzed Jacque. My office door opened almost before I'd put down the phone, and she swept in, notepad in hand, and dragged up a chair. I slowly shook my head.

"What?"

"Nothing. Look, I need you to call Congressman Harper's office. See if you can make an appointment for me to see him early tomorrow morning. I don't care what time, just get me in. Just make it sound casual. If he asks why I want to see him, tell him you don't know, but you think it's something to do with my father."

She made a few notes on her pad, then looked up at me expectantly.

"I need someone to look into the financing of that new strip mall up on McCallie. Maybe you can get Rogers to check into it. He needs the experience. Tell him that I need to know who owns it, who put up the money, who owns the businesses, and that I'll need to know all of that before I go see Harper. If Rogers runs into a roadblock, and he might, have Tim give him a hand with it. And... no, that's it for now. I need some quiet time. I need to think. Keep the wolves away for an hour or so. Urgent calls only, okay?"

"Of course. But please don't forget to call Judge Strange and Larry Soames. Can I get you some coffee?"

"No, but thanks. Just make sure I'm not disturbed. I'll buzz you if I need you, or when I'm done."

She nodded, got up, and left the room, leaving me to enjoy a moment or two of quiet solitude.

I put my feet up on the desk, closed my eyes, and let the thoughts whirl around in my head. Two seconds later I realized I needed to talk to Charlie Maxwell. *Dammit.* I dropped my feet back to the floor and dialed the number Dr. Willard had given me. It rang and rang. I was just about to hang up when she answered.

"Hello." The voice was low, sexy. She made that single word sound like an invitation you couldn't refuse.

"Charlotte Maxwell?"

"Yes, speaking."

"Ms. Maxwell. My name is Harry Starke. I'm a private investigator—"

"Yes, I know. Dr. Willard called me. He said you might call."

"Oh, okay. Well, I was there, on the bridge, when Tabitha.... Well, you know. I wonder if you could spare a few minutes, to talk. How about I buy you coffee?"

"Well, I suppose, but—"

"Great. How about Starbucks at the Read House. In thirty minutes?"

There was a moment of silence, then: "Well, okay. Thirty minutes. How will I know you?"

"I'll be the guy in the black leather jacket. See you in thirty."

I hung up the phone, jumped to my feet, and walked out into the main office. Jacque looked up expectantly.

"Sorry," I told her. "Gotta go out for a few. I'll be back as soon as I can. Take messages."

9

I arrived at Starbucks just before Charlotte did. Some years ago—many years ago—there was a song called, "Did You Ever See a Dream Walking?" Corny as hell, right? But at that moment I knew exactly what the guy who wrote it meant. Charlotte Maxwell was a dream, a vision. Tall, at least six feet, slim, dressed in tight-fitting black jeans, a black silk blouse, white leather shell jacket, and high heels, her dark brown hair was swept back from her high forehead and tied in a ponytail. Her eyes were huge, the color of pale jade. *Contacts?*

As far as I could tell, she wore little makeup—she didn't need to—just a hint of pale rose lipstick. This girl could have stepped right off the runway. Every head in the room turned to look at her, and it was easy to tell that she was used to the attention.

I stood, waved to her, and waited as she stalked across the room toward me. Even her walk attracted attention. I slid out a chair for her, and she flowed into it. *How do they do that?*

"What can I get for you, Charlotte?" I asked.

"Call me Charlie. Everyone does. I'll have a tall iced coffee, please." There was that voice again.

"So, Mr. Detective." She looked at me, thoughtfully, as I put the drink down on the table in front of her. "You said you wanted to talk to me about Tab. What would you like to know?"

"Let's start with how well you knew her."

She leaned her elbows on the table, hands folded over one the other under her chin, and looked into my eyes. My heart almost stopped.

"Oh, I knew her well, very well. We were like... sisters." The voice was deep, not quite husky.

"Tell me about her."

"She was a very sweet girl. Gentle, giving, loving—she was my best friend. What else is there to tell?"

"What was she doing in a sleazy downtown bar at midnight? What was her relationship with the two gang-bangers I saw her with in that bar? Why was she scared out of her wits? Why would she take a dive off the bridge? How about those questions, just for starters, Charlie?"

She looked at me, her chin still resting on the backs of her hands, and then she leaned back in her chair, shrugged, turned her head, and looked away. Her mood was pensive, her expression passive. For a long moment she was silent, then she looked me directly in the eye.

"I... don't... know." She didn't say it aloud. She mouthed it, her mouth exaggerating the form of each word.

"But you were her best friend," I said. "If anyone would know what was going on with her, you would. Think. Was she in trouble? Was there anything different about her these last few weeks?"

She thought for a moment, staring at me. I was beginning to feel a little uncomfortable.

"Hmmm.... Well, maybe. She certainly didn't like it when Michael dumped her."

"Michael? Do you know his last name?"

"Falk. Michael Falk. They'd been seeing each other for about a year. I thought it was serious. Obviously he didn't think so."

Michael Falk. I made a mental note of the name.

"Where can I find him? Do you have a phone number?"

"I don't know. I have no idea where he lives, and I don't know his phone number, but I do know he works for some politician. As a speechwriter, I think. They were all hot and heavy for a while, Tab and him, then all of a sudden... well, you know, that was it. I haven't seen him for weeks."

I perked up. "Politician? Any idea who?"

"Oh yes. Gordon Harper."

I smiled to myself. "Go on."

"Well, after Michael left her, she seemed quiet, agitated, and unhappy. I put all that down to the breakup, but then I began to see less and less of her. We used to be joined at the hip, even when she was seeing someone, but that all changed about three weeks ago, when Michael...." She broke off, eyes watering. "Why did she do it, Mr. Starke? She had beauty, money, everything." She leaned forward, reached out, and put her hand on mine. This time my heart did stop.

I let her hand stay where it was and swallowed. "Charlie, I know she was in public relations. Her father told me that. But who did she work for, and what exactly did she do all day, every day?"

She withdrew her hand, picked up her coffee, leaned

back, took a sip, and then looked at me through lowered eyelids.

Damn.

"I don't know who she worked for. Some company out of New York, I think, but I never did ask her the name. I wasn't interested. I think she may have freelanced for them. She was able to come and go pretty much as she pleased. I do know she had several major clients, regulars, who took up a lot of her time. She spent a lot of the time on the computer doing research: Facebook, Twitter, you know how it is. And she had a good time. She had a great social life, was a good golfer, played tennis, and she had lots and lots of friends. She traveled some, to New York, Chicago, and Boston, Washington. She stayed busy."

All the time she was talking, she was gazing at me through lowered lashes.

I'd had enough. She was intimidating. Hot as hell, but intimidating. I had to get out of there before I said something I'd regret, but before I did....

"How about these, Charlie? What do you know about them?" One by one, I laid the card, the key, and finally the pendant out in front her. I watched her eyes, looking for the tiniest reaction: nothing.

She touched the card with the forefinger of her right hand. "I've never seen this before."

"What about the phone number? Do you recognize it?"

She shook her head.

"The key?"

She shrugged, then shook her head.

"What about the pendant?"

She stared at it, hesitated. It wasn't much, and if I hadn't been looking for it, I wouldn't have noticed.

"No."

"Charlie...."

"What?"

"Come on, Charlie. You're not a good liar. I can tell. You've seen it before. Haven't you?"

She stared at me, for a long moment, then nodded.

"What does it mean, Charlie? Where did she get it?"

"I've no idea what it means, probably nothing. It was a gift."

"A gift? Who gave it to her, Charlie? When?"

"It wasn't too long ago, maybe six months. Perhaps a little longer. I don't know who gave it to her. She never talked about it. I did ask her, but all she'd say was that a friend had given it to her. She didn't say who that friend was."

"Why didn't you want to tell me about it?"

Again, she hesitated. "I don't know. Tab was... She... I don't know, Mr. Starke, I didn't want to... get her into trouble?" She said it as if it were a question. Then she lowered her eyes and looked down at her coffee. She knew something. I was sure of it, but I had a feeling I wasn't going to get any more out of her than I already had, at least not now. Maybe another time.

She looked up at me. There were tears in her eyes. "Do you think it had something to do with...?"

I shook my head, gathered the items up, and put them back in my pocket. "Probably not, but she was wearing it when they found her. It's kind of unique."

She wiped her eyes with a tissue she took from her pocket, then seemed to gather herself together. She straightened, sitting up very erect, her hands folded one atop the other on the table. Then she smiled at me. It was a heart-breaking smile.

"One more thing, Charlie, what do *you* do for a living?"

She looked a little taken aback by the question, hesitated for a second. "Me? I'm in computers. I'm a systems analyst, among other things."

"What other things?"

She smiled, looked at me through half-closed eyes. "Come now, Harry. A girl has to keep some secrets, right?"

I took out my wallet, handed her my card. "Okay. That will do it for now, Charlie, and thank you. You've been very helpful. I need to go, catch up on a few things. If you think of anything else, please give me a call."

She looked down at me when she stood up, her eyes wide. They were like vast pools of emerald water flecked with gold.

Contacts, I thought. *Gotta be.*

"Will I see you again?"

It wasn't the question that took my breath away; it was the way she asked it: full of promise.

"Maybe. If I need to talk to you again. Goodbye, Charlie."

I took out my phone and dialed. She took the hint and left me sitting there, staring after her. I waited a moment, then followed her out onto the street, just in time to see the back of her as she turned right into the multi-story parking lot.

As cold as it was that afternoon, I was sweating. The air outside was like cool white wine, and I gulped as much of it into me as I could.

Later I sat in the car, thinking about the interview. It was hard to get Charlie off my mind, and I was having a tough time trying to figure her out. One thing I was sure of: she knew more than she pretended to. I'd need to talk to Charlie Maxwell again.

10

I got back to the office right after four. Both Jacque and young Mike Rogers stood when I walked in. Mike looked excited. I pulled a wry face. I had a lot on my mind and didn't need to lose track of it. I needed some quiet time, time to think. Nevertheless, as I swept through the main office and opened the door to my inner sanctum, I waved for them to follow. I flung myself down in my chair and crossed my feet on top of the desk.

"Sit down, both of you. Talk to me."

Rogers sat.

Jacque didn't. She said, "You have an appointment with Congressman Harper at ten tomorrow. He was reluctant, but I persuaded him. I wouldn't be late, if I were you. He might cancel. That's all I have. I'll leave you two to talk."

"Oh, Jacque...."

She paused, turned. "Yes?"

"Have Ronnie and Tim come in, please. Tell them they'll need to take notes."

She nodded and closed the door behind her. I looked at Rogers. He was excited, couldn't wait.

"Hold on, son. Let's wait for Ronnie and Tim."

Tim Clarke is my computer guy. He handles all things to do with the Internet, including operating and maintaining the company website. He also handles background checks and skip searches, and a whole lot more besides. He can find people, addresses, phone numbers, you name it. He's a geek, and he looks like one. Tall, skinny, glasses, twenty-five years old. He's perhaps the most useful and effective tool in my bag.

Ronnie Hall handles my white-collar investigations. He's been around since I opened the office. His background is in banking. He has an MSc in finance from the London School of Economics.

"Sit down, guys. Before we begin, Tim, did you have any luck tracing that number?

"The phone was purchased at Walmart, Gunbarrel branch, on December third last year. That's all I have. The security tapes are on a loop."

I nodded. I wasn't surprised. Sometimes it works, sometimes it doesn't.

"Okay, Mike. Let me have it."

"Green Tree Strip Mall..."

I laughed out loud, couldn't help it. I didn't mean to interrupt the boy, but Green Tree? That was hilarious. Shady really was coming up in the world. "Sorry, Mike. Go on."

"The financing for the construction of the mall was provided by the Horstel Group, a merchant bank registered and located in Dubai. The mall is owned by Stanwood Properties of Atlanta, a company specializing in real estate investments. The company officers are," he paused, grinning at me across the desk, "Lester Tree and Henry Gold. The tax records list Lester Tree as the COO. Stanwood Properties is owned by Goodwin and Associates, a shell corporation registered in the Cayman Islands. Goodwin and Associates are, in turn, owned by Nickajack Investments, another shell corporation, also registered in the Cayman Islands. As far as I can tell, there is no Goodwin and there are no associates and, so far, I can find nothing at all about Nickajack Investments."

I scanned my notes. "Wow," I murmured, more to myself than to Rogers. "It takes your breath away. There's no way it's legal. Why would they need to hide it away like that? It's just a little strip mall, for God's sake." I looked up at him. "Nickajack? As in Nickajack Lake, Nickajack Dam?"

He nodded and grinned at me. "Coincidence?"

"Not likely. That name is unique to Chattanooga. Someone is thumbing their nose at the establishment and, considering his connection to Tree, that would most likely be the enigmatic Congressman Harper. I wonder who's financing the financier, Horstel? Any idea?"

"No, sir. You know the banking system in Dubai: tight as f... ah, sorry. That almost slipped out."

"No problem, son. I've heard and said a whole lot worse. Go on."

"Dubai's banking system." He looked at Ronnie and grinned. "Dubai's banking system is as tight as... well, it's tight."

"Okay," I said. "So although the Green Tree Mall does not appear to be *actually* owned by the inimitable Mr. Tree, he was telling the truth. He is in fact the man behind the business.... Nah! There's no way in hell. I don't believe it. I wouldn't trust Shady with a dime of my money, and neither would anyone else who's known him for more than thirty seconds. He's a front man, bought and paid for. By Harper, I wouldn't doubt. We know, at least we think we do, that they're somehow connected."

I leaned back in my chair and stared up at the ceiling. My mind was a whirl. I looked at my notes, then at young Mike Rogers.

"Okay, Mike, it's a good start, but we need to know more. Ronnie, I want you to take the lead on this, but keep Mike in the loop; he's made a good start. Keep digging, both of you. I want to know more about Horstel, Nickajack, Stanwood, and Goodwin, and let's take it a step farther. See what you can find out about Old Man Harper's Foundation. What's its purpose? Where does it get its money? How's the money being used? Who's responsible for its operation? Dig deep. I want to know everything there is to know about it. I want to know more about that foundation than Harper does."

I paused for a moment, thinking about what I was going to say next.

"Tim, I want you to dig into Tabitha Willard. Find out everything you can about her, especially where she got her money from; it wasn't from her old man. I also want you to look into someone else for me: Charlotte Maxwell, goes by the name of Charlie. Here's her phone number, but do *not* call her. I don't want her to know that we're looking at her. Be discreet. Find out where she lives, what she does for a living, her finances, everything. And there's one more thing I'd like you to look into: Michael Falk. He was Tabitha Willard's boyfriend. He works for Harper, but he hasn't been seen for a couple of weeks. Soon as you can, okay?"

"You got it, Mr. Starke."

"Okay, that's it. Let me know when you have something."

I was about to let them go when I had another thought. I reached into my jacket pocket and fished out the pendant. I tossed it over the desk. Tim caught it, looked at it, and then looked at me questioningly.

"See what you can find out about that," I told him. "I have a feeling it means something, but I have no idea what. Let me know if you find anything. Take a photo of it and let me have it back."

He took out his cell, snapped a shot, and handed the pendant back to me.

They rose and walked out of the office, and Mike closed the door behind him. I leaned back once more and stared up at the ceiling. I let my mind wander. Soon it was filled with the shadows of the past several days, twisting and turning.

Charlie Maxwell? What is it with her? Beautiful. Wow! You can say that again. Beautiful! Was she coming on to me? I grinned at the thought, then pushed it out of my mind.

What about Michael Falk? Need to find him, talk to him.

Why did he dump Tabitha? Guys don't dump girls like her.

Who did she work for?

He works for Harper, so that also connects Tabitha to Harper. The plot thickens.

Does Harper own any of the offshore dummy corporations? If so, which ones?

Follow the money!

Why are the finances of the foundation so murky?

Is there any connection between the foundation and the mall? Is Harper connected to the mall? If so, how, and why?

Well, maybe tomorrow will shed a little light on what the congressman is up to.

Maybe I'll shake his tree. Hah, good one.

The pendant... what does it mean? Probably nothing. So why am I so hung up on it?

What about the key? The business card? Why was the number disconnected right after I called it?

I sighed, opened the center drawer of my desk and took out a legal pad. It was time to make a list, put things in perspective.

1. Little Billy is spending a lot of money.
2. Why are the Feds looking at him?
3. The key. What does it fit?
4. The business card?
5. The phone number?
6. Charlie Maxwell?
7. Michael Falk?
8. Harper + Tree?
9. Offshore companies?
10. The foundation?
11. The mall?
12. WHY DID SHE JUMP?

I picked up the pad, leaned back in my chair, and stared at the list. It was depressingly short, and I had no answers except maybe for the last one, and that one I sure as hell didn't like.

I tossed the pad onto the desk with a sigh and looked at my watch. It was time to go home. No, it wasn't. I still had a couple of calls to make. *Dammit.*

I made the calls to Judge Strange and Larry Soames.

Strange is a good contact. You never know when you're going to need a friendly federal judge, so it's good to have one on your team. All he wanted to know was the status of a case I had Heather working on. I quickly brought him up to speed. It was going to take a few days longer than I had previously thought. He was a bit put out, but I promised him lunch and we ended the call on a happy note. I really like the old boy.

Larry Soames wanted to hire me. A routine divorce case. The husband was having an affair. Soames needed proof of infidelity. Bread and butter stuff. I never turn those away. I handed him over to Jacque. Had her do the paperwork, go get a check for the retainer, and then put Heather on it. I was done for the day.

11

It was just after four thirty when I left the office. I needed to get to Greenlife to purchase some ingredients for the evening meal. I was looking forward to it. I like to cook, although no one ever believes I do. I find it relaxing, and I'm pretty good at it. I had a nice bottle of Riesling chilling in the wine cooler, and I had Mary, my housekeeper, go in and lay the table. That's something I *do* hate doing.

I had the butcher cut me a couple of generous salmon steaks, then I picked out two nice potatoes and the ingredients for an Asian salad.

It was already dark when I arrived home. The view from my living room window was stunning, as always. The lights on the opposite side of the Tennessee were twinkling like it was Christmas. The Thrasher Bridge was a ribbon of lights; Chattanooga was heading home for the night. The sky was a deep purple and there was a light mist on the surface of the river, and I couldn't help but think of that poor girl tumbling down into the freezing water. I shuddered and shook my head.

She wouldn't have felt anything, with the cold, and she'd gone headfirst from a height. She must have died instantly, or near enough.... Neck snapped....

I jerked myself out of it, looked at the table set for two. Nice. I smiled, nodded to myself, and headed for the kitchen. I put the potatoes in the oven and prepared the salad. I looked at my watch. There was just time enough for a shower before Kate arrived.

Fifteen minutes later, I was dressed in a pair of lightweight tan slacks, a pale pink (the associate at the store called it grenadine) golf shirt, and a pair of comfortable Italian loafers. Hah, now I looked like I belonged in my apartment rather than being there to rob it.

I had just put the salmon in the oven when Kate arrived. She rang the bell and let herself in.

"Wow." She walked across the living room into the kitchen, looking at me the whole way, and after she'd kissed me lightly on the lips, she took a step back for another look. I grinned at her.

"I like it," she said. "You should dress like this more often. I do like the rough, tough look; it's very... masculine, but this is much nicer." She slipped out of her coat, tossed it over the back of one of the barstools at the breakfast bar, and perched on the one next to it. She liked to watch me cook.

"You look pretty good yourself," I said.

Geez, what an understatement. She's gorgeous!

Now I have to tell you, Kate always looks good, even at work. She dresses well, and always for the occasion, so I guess tonight must have been pretty special. She was wearing a woolen dress that was cut five inches above the knee and showed a lot of thigh, seated as she was on the stool.

I nodded toward the bottle and glasses. "Would you like to pour the wine?"

She did. She reached out, took the bottle, poured a small quantity into both glasses, swirled hers around the glass, put it to her nose and breathed, nodded. She took a sip, nodded again, looked at me, tilted her head to one side, and said, "Nice one, Harry."

I watched her out of the corner of my eye as I put the food on the plates. Inwardly, I shook my head, unable to believe my good fortune.

The meal was quick and easy. I served the lightly grilled salmon steaks with a baked potato garnished with lemon garlic butter sauce and an Asian salad: celery and parsley leaves; radish, alfalfa and bean sprouts, scallions, and Asian pear coated in a light lemon–rice wine vinaigrette. The wine was cool and delicious. The company was... let's just say better than any man, let alone me, deserved.

We ate the meal almost in silence. When we were done, we finished the wine and I made coffee. No coffee maker this time; I used a French press.

"So, what did you do today?" she asked. We were still at the table, relaxing.

"Quite a lot. As you know, I went to see Willard and Shady. After lunch with you, I went back to the office and called my father."

She raised her eyebrows.

I nodded, and then continued, "I told you I needed a reason for my visit to Harper tomorrow morning. He supplied it. I have a check from him, a donation to Harper's campaign fund. It was all I could think of. I also met with Charlotte Maxwell this afternoon, had coffee with her. It was interesting, to say the least."

"Tell me. What did you think of her?"

"Well, as you know, she's beautiful and she's intelligent, and... and, I'm not sure, but I think she came onto me."

Kate sat back in her chair and grinned at me. "Do tell."

I smiled at her, sheepishly. "Well, she was obviously upset, about Tabitha."

"And you took advantage of her. You dog, Harry Starke." She was joking, I could tell.

"No, Kate. You know me better than that. Maybe I was wrong. It was just a moment. She put her hand on mine and looked at me. That was all, but..."

"Harry." She was serious now. "I'm sure you're right. She probably did come onto you; she's the type who would. But you'd better be careful. You know what I mean? Maybe I should go with you next time, if there is a next time."

I did know what she meant. She was talking about ethics, and especially entrapment.

"Oh, there'll be a next time. I need to know a whole lot more about both her and Tabitha Willard. But don't worry. I can handle her. By the way, the boyfriend's name is Michael Falk, but Charlie seems to think he did in fact dump her, just like you said. According to her, she hasn't seen him for several weeks."

"Charlie, is it? My, aren't we friendly, though?"

"Hah, that's just what everyone calls her. First thing she said when I introduced myself."

"What else did she say?"

"Not a whole lot of anything, now I think about it. To be honest, I had a tough job reading the woman. There's something about her that I'm not quite getting. Oh, and contrary to what she told you, she does know about the pendant, but she was reluctant to talk about it. She said Tabitha had received it as a gift, some six months back. That was about all I could get out of her."

I thought back to the interview, trying to dredge up what I'd missed: nothing would come.

"She has an air about her. She was... dreamy," I continued. "I don't mean she was high; nothing like that. Just... well... dreamy is the only word I can think of. Even more strange is how little she seems to know about Tabitha Willard. If you live with someone you usually know everything there is to know about them, but no. And yet she claims they were best friends. I asked all the questions. She said Tabitha was in public relations, but that was all she knew. She didn't know who she worked for, who her clients were, what she did for them, or how she spent her days, other than that she was some kind of freelancer, came and went almost as she pleased. Hell, now that I think about it, the whole interview was a total waste of time. The only solid piece of information I got out of it was Michael Falk's name, and that he worked for Harper... You wanna go sit on the sofa, look at the view?"

"Sure. I love this place, Harry."

"By the way," I said, as we made ourselves comfortable, "you may well be right about Harper's shady dealings and the foundation. I don't have much yet. Not enough to draw any real conclusions, but I have Ronnie looking into it. I told him to dig deep. As soon as I have something, I'll let you know."

She nodded, pensively. Her mood had changed. The time for conversation was over.

We sat together on the couch for more than an hour, looking out over the river, enjoying the view, making small talk. We could see the lights on the Thrasher Bridge. There was a half moon, and the light from it turned the surface of the river into a vast blanket of shimmering, undulating silver. She was curled up beside me, her head on my chest. It was a beautiful moment. Not a rare moment, because we sat together like that often, but the sort of moment I always enjoyed.

Suddenly she sat up, threw back her hair, and leaned in close. I could feel her breasts against my chest as she kissed me. A gentle, lingering kiss that silently told me all of the things I'd always wanted to hear her say. Then she stood, turned to face me, stretched her arms high over her head like some huge tawny cat, then took my hands in hers and pulled.

"Let's go to bed, Harry."

12

Congressman Harper had a suite of offices on the top floor of a downtown high-rise on Market Street. I found a handy meter, shoved in a half-dozen quarters, entered the building, and took the elevator to the top floor. It was quiet up there. Plush carpets, expensive furniture and artwork. The congressman had a corner office overlooking Market Street and Lookout Mountain. Nice. I entered the reception area and handed my card to the smartly dressed young man behind the desk. He punched a button on the phone and said, "Mr. Starke is here, sir."

He listened to whoever was on the other end for a moment, then hung up and looked at me. "The congressman will see you now, Mr. Starke. This way, please."

He showed me through a heavy walnut door, , then closed it behind us. The door squeaked slightly as he pulled it shut.

And there he was, a benign portrait of the quintessential politician.

At sixty-two, Gordon Harper was the picture of health and well-being: white hair, bald pate, twinkling blue eyes, and a smile that even Joe Biden would envy. Those teeth must have cost a fortune. Seated behind one of those metal desks with a glass top you could see right through, he was wearing a short-sleeved sports shirt and a white belt over black slacks. His only jewelry was a ring and a wristwatch, a slim, understated gold Breitling that nestled unobtrusively within the thick weft of dark hair on his left wrist. If Little Billy was a crook, he sure as hell didn't look it.

The next thing I noticed was the man standing with his back to the window. Shaved head, shiny, small gold hoops in both ear lobes, no sideburns, just a black mustache that circled his mouth and joined a sharp pointed beard. He reminded me of the old-time movie star Anton LaVey, or maybe an evil wizard, only this guy was six foot two and could easily have passed for Secret Service, which I'm sure he wasn't. He was too well dressed. No off-the-rack suit for him. The one he was wearing was expensive, tailored, and... was that a slight bulge under his left arm? He stood with his legs apart and his arms hanging loose in front of him, hands clasped together one over the other.

Harper caught me looking at the man, lowered the china coffee cup he'd been holding to say, "Jackson Hope is my private secretary, Mr. Starke." He turned in his seat. "You can go, Jackson. Just stay close, in case I need you."

I'm not sure what he meant by that, but I'm pretty sure he wouldn't need him to take dictation. Anyway, he set the coffee cup down on the desk and looked at me through narrowed eyes, brow wrinkled in a frown.

"I've heard of you, Mr. Starke. Who around this town hasn't? You're Judge Sharpe's blue-eyed boy."

It was a veiled joke, I was sure, but I wasn't amused. The look on my face must have told him so, because he smiled.

"I'm sorry, that was uncalled for. I apologize. What can I do for you, Mr. Starke? What is it that you couldn't talk to me about over the phone?" He said "apologize," but I could tell he didn't mean it. This was a man who never apologized for anything.

"Call me Harry, Congressman. My father asked me to call on you. I believe you know him, right?"

He nodded. "Why didn't he come himself? Why send you?"

"Couple of reasons. One, he's extremely busy—he spends most of his time in court—and two, he figures he's too high profile. He said he wanted discretion."

"He's high profile... and you're not? That's funny, Harry. Very funny."

"Well, he's looking for favors; I'm not. He asked me to stop by to give you this, a contribution to your upcoming campaign. He also hinted that there might a donation to the Harper Foundation." I handed him the check for $2700. "He also said something about making friends in high places, whatever that means."

He took the check, looked at it, put it down in front him, and carefully adjusted its position on the desk until it was perfectly horizontal.

The man was OCD.

"I'm not sure I know what to make of this, Mr. Starke. I don't do *quid pro quo*." He started to push the check toward me.

"No, sir, I'm sure you don't, and that was not the intention. Your politics are his politics. You win; he wins. It's as simple as that."

"Are you talking tort reform, Harry?" he asked, so quietly I could barely hear him. He thought I was recording him. "Because if you are, I can't help you."

I shrugged but said nothing. Then I got it. I could have banged my head against the wall. The bastard was recording me.

I grinned at him and shook my head. "Absolutely not. It's not meant as a bribe, Congressman. Look at the dollar value. It's the maximum donation allowed by an individual. If I were going to offer you a bribe, I wouldn't do it here, and it would be for a whole lot more than $2,700. That's a nice ring, by the way."

"Why thank you." He held his hand out for me to see it. I leaned forward to get a closer look.

"Yes. Very nice. What does it mean?"

"I have no idea. It was a gift from a very dear friend." Then he relaxed, settled himself back in his chair, and looked benignly at me across the expanse of polished glass: the check still front and center thereon.

"Well," he said, with a smile as fake as three-dollar bill, "if that's all, then, Mr. Starke. I, too, am a busy man. Please thank August for me. Tell him we need to get together for lunch sometime, maybe even nine holes at the club. Now, if you don't mind...."

Okay. Now, let's see if the seed I planted in Shady's office yesterday has born any fruit. It's time to throw a little bait into the waters.

"I met a friend of yours yesterday, Congressman. Lester Tree. At least he said he was a friend. Do you know him well?"

He gave no reaction, other than to wrinkle his brow in

question. "Lester Tree? Never heard of him." He straightened up in his chair and reached for his coffee cup. I couldn't help but notice the slight shake of his hand as he put it to his lips and sipped. It was enough. I think he was surprised when he realized the cup was already empty.

So Shady *had* made the call, and Harper was ready for me. He was good, must be a poker player: no tells, stoic, even, but there was something different about his body language. He wasn't quite as at ease as he had been just moments ago.

"Oh, I could have sworn..." I said, with a smile, the meaning of which I tried to make very clear. "Well, maybe I was wrong... but he did say *Congressman* Harper. Funny, that. Well, never mind. I'll let you get back to what you were doing. Have a great day, sir." I rose to my feet, turned toward the door, stopped and said, "Would you like me to send Jackson in? I'm sure he'll be waiting right outside."

I could almost feel the look he gave me.

"No, that's all right. Thank you. You take care, you hear? And you have a good day, too."

There was an edge to the words, but I smiled to myself all the way down to the lobby and out into the winter sunshine. *Now that was easy.*

I had wanted to ask him about Michael Falk, but I could tell that the interview was over. He was already antsy, and I really didn't know how to do it without making him even more so—*discretion, Kate said*—so I decided to let it go, for now.

I got into my car and pulled away down Market Street, checking my rearview mirrors as I did so. Again, I smiled to myself. Five or six parking meters to my rear, a small silver Honda SUV pulled out behind me and entered the stream of traffic. I turned right on Fourth, then right on Georgia, and from there I drove to my office. As I pulled into my parking space, the Honda cruised by and then turned left on East Eighth.

So, I must have caused ripples in the water after all.

13

It was eleven o'clock that same morning when I walked into my office. Everyone turned away from whatever they were doing to look at me. It registered, but what really caught my eye was Mike—or, the state of his face. I stopped in front of his desk. His nose was in one of those aluminum splints and the flesh around it was almost black. He had a black eye, a split lip, and there was a nasty-looking scrape on his right cheek.

"What the hell happened to you?"

He looked sheepishly up at me and tried to smile—it didn't work—and then he said, through lips he could barely move, "I got in a fight, sort of."

Now that was the most ridiculous thing I'd ever heard. Mike couldn't fight his way out of a wet paper bag. He's twenty-four years old, stands no more than five feet ten inches tall, and has to run around in the shower to get wet. I'm not saying he's a wimp, but he sure as hell is no street fighter. Hell, even a big girl could do him some serious damage.

"What happened, Mike? You have a run in with someone's jealous boyfriend?"

He smiled, winced, and then shook his head. "No, sir. It happened up on McCallie, at the mall."

My eyes went wide. *What the hell?*

"Come to my office. Tell me about it."

He followed me in and closed the door.

"Sit there. Can you handle a coffee?"

He shook his head.

"Well, I've got to have some. Just sit tight for a minute."

I went back out into the outer office and punched the button on the coffee machine: Dark Italian Roast, black, no sugar.

"I could have done that for you."

"Yes, Jacque. I know. But I don't pay you to wait on me, though you do a great job of it. But thanks. I think you'd better come and sit in on this one. You, too, Bob."

Bob Ryan, my lead investigator, shoved the papers he was working on to one side and rose to his feet. Now, Bob, unlike Mike Rogers, is a street fighter: six feet two and two-hundred-forty pounds of solid muscle, a marine with a fondness for baseball bats. You don't screw around with Bob Ryan.

I flopped into my seat behind my desk. Bob and Jacque sat together on the loveseat.

I looked across the desk at Mike. He looked pathetic.

"Let's have it, Mike. Tell me what happened and tell me what the hell you were you doing there on your own."

Again, he gave me that cow-eyed look. "I went to the mall last night. I wanted to check it out, see if I could learn anything. You said to keep checking, right?"

"I didn't mean for you to go poking about. Mike, you're

not a field investigator. That's Bob and Heather's job. They're good at it, and they have years of experience. They also know how to look after themselves. You don't. You're here to learn, not to get yourself killed. What did you get yourself into?"

"I'm sorry, Mr. Starke. I wanted to see what I could find out. So I went. The office was dark—at least I couldn't see any lights on. The two clothing stores were closed. The cigar store, the restaurant, and the gym were all open. I went into the cigar store first. There was no one inside except for the guy behind the counter, an overweight dude who looked like he could barely stand up, must have been at least four hundred pounds." He paused, licked his damaged lip.

"I wandered around in there for a minute, then I asked him who owned the place."

I interrupted him, "Just like that? You asked just like that, out of the blue? No 'Hey, nice to meet you?' No conversation? That's..." I shook my head. "Go on, son."

"He was really nice, Mr. Starke. Didn't tell me a whole lot, just that Lester Tree owned it, and that's all he knew. He didn't know anything about the other businesses so I bought a cigar and left."

I interrupted him again. "And as soon as you did, he made a call. Go on."

"Well, then I went into the gym. Asked about membership, how I could join and all. I hadn't been in there more'n a minute when someone tapped me on the shoulder. It was a big black dude, and he had a sidekick with him, a smaller man in a weird-looking suit. The big guy took my arm and dragged me out into the parking lot, and then into the office unit. Mr. Tree was there. He wanted to know what I was up to, and who I was working for. I told him I just wanted to join the gym. He said he didn't believe me. I didn't tell him anything, Mr. Starke. I swear it. I kept my mouth shut. He doesn't know I work for you. Anyway, finally he told the big guy to take me out and teach me a lesson, rough me up a little, and..." He shrugged, dropped his head, and stared at his shoes.

"It's okay, Mike. It was a good lesson. One you won't forget, ever. From now on, you leave the field work to us, okay?"

He nodded.

"Still want to be a PI?" I grinned across the desk at him.

He looked up. "More than ever."

"Okay, go on. Get outa here. Go back to digging but use the Internet and the phone this time."

I leaned back in my chair and watched him close the door behind him.

"Seems like the kid hit a nerve," Bob said.

"That he did."

"Let's go talk to Tree." Bob's voice was deep, almost a growl, menacing even when he's being nice, which he rarely ever was.

I thought for a minute, then reluctantly shook my head. There's no one I'd rather have with me in a tough situation than Bob, but I had something else in mind; something that, if it went wrong, would get me into serious trouble. I didn't want anyone else involved. Especially not my staff.

"No, Bob. It's better I do this alone. I don't want you getting into trouble, not at this stage anyway."

He looked at me through narrowed eyes.

"I know. Tell you what. If I need help, I'll call. Okay?"

It wasn't okay. I could see it in his eyes. But he nodded anyway.

"You got it." He got up. So did Jacque. They left me alone with my thoughts.

I sat there for a moment, pondered about what I was about to do, then opened my desk drawer. I retrieved half a dozen heavy-duty plastic cable ties, already looped, and my expandable baton. With a flick of the wrist, I can open it up to sixteen inches and it becomes a weapon to be feared by even the toughest banger. Closed, it's the next best thing to a knuckle-duster. Hold it tight in your fist, and your hand becomes a sledgehammer. I put it in my jacket pocket, checked the load of the nine, and made sure there was one in the chamber. Then I made a quick call to Kate.

I gave her a quick rundown of my meeting with Harper, but I didn't tell her what I was about to do. Then I looked around the office one last time and walked out into the cold afternoon air.

14

It was almost two o'clock that afternoon when I headed out from the office. Jacque looked worried. She knew something was up. Bob looked up from his computer, winked, and put the thumb and little finger of his right hand to his ear and mouthed, "Call me." Mike looked as if he was about to throw up, but I smiled at him and winked.

"Back soon, guys," I told them. "Hold down the fort."

I drove slowly down Georgia, going over what I was about to do. It wasn't the best plan I'd ever come up with, but it would have to do. There was no way I was going to let Tree get away with hammering one of my people, especially a kid like Mike.

It was five after two when I drove into the rear parking lot of the mall. There were a few cars, but no people. I eased on around to the front and parked a few feet to the left of Shady's office door and the tinted window. I got out of the car, locked the doors, and walked to the office door.

I took a deep breath and thumbed the bell, then stepped to one side so I couldn't be seen through the peephole. I took the baton from my belt, made a fist around it, and waited. A minute later the door opened. Just a little. I hit it with my shoulder, and the guy behind it went through the same stumble-and-fall routine as a couple days ago, but this time, before he could recover, I was on him. I hammered him upside the head with the closed baton. He didn't see it coming and went down like he'd been hit by a truck. It only took a couple seconds to secure his hands with one of the ties, and then I ran down the passageway and didn't stop until I hit Shady's office door. The frame shattered. I almost fell through the opening into his office, but I managed to keep my balance.

Surprised? You bet they were. Two bounding strides and I had smacked Duvon over the head with the baton. He went down, howling in pain. Out of the corner of my eye, I saw Gold reaching inside his jacket. I was too quick for him. I flipped the baton, across the room like a Frisbee, back handed. It flew over the desk, barely missing Shady's head, spinning end over end. Gold didn't have a chance; the stainless-steel butt hit him full on the nose, which burst like a ripe tomato. He coughed once; blood spurted from the damaged snout, sprayed over Tree's back and onto his desk. Gold howled, grabbed his nose with both hands, and sank slowly to his knees, moaning quietly.

I pulled the M&P9 and leveled it at Tree. "Don't you move so much as a finger, Shady."

I stepped quickly around the desk, keeping an eye on Shady, and slipped a tie over Duvon's wrists. Then I went to Gold, bent down, felt inside his jacket, and relieved him of a 9 mm semi-automatic. I placed it on the corner of the desk, as far away from Tree as I could. Then, with my free hand, I slipped a tie over Gold's wrists and pulled it tight. Next, I picked up the baton and slipped it into my jacket pocket. Then I turned and faced Tree, who was still sitting at his desk. He hadn't moved a muscle. His face had turned a funny color, but he leaned back in his chair and smiled up at me, only it wasn't a smile, it was a teeth-bared grimace.

"What can I do for you this time, Mr. Starke?" It was barely a whisper.

"I want to know why your boys beat the shit out of my intern."

"You mean the nosy kid, blond, with pimples? He stuck his nose somewhere he shouldn't, an' he got caught. Henry here," he nodded down at the still sobbing Gold, "heard that he was asking questions about me in the gym. Simple. He needed a lesson. I had Duvon teach it to him, bust his nose for him, teach him to keep it out of where it don't belong. He'll get over it. Hell, who never had a busted nose before?"

"Okay, Tree. Listen up. The boy needs surgery, and you're going to pay for it."

"The hell you say."

"The hell I do say. You don't pay up, I'll put a cap through your knee. I'll put you on sticks for the rest of your days. You don't think I'll do it? Try me."

He looked at me for a long time. His eyes flicked back and forth, between mine and the front end of the nine, thinking. Then he looked up at the ceiling, sighed, looked again across the desk at me, at the gun in my hand, rolled his eyes, leaned forward, pulled open a drawer and took out a checkbook.

"How much?"

"You gotta be joking. You're gonna write me a check. How stupid d'you think I am? Cash, Shady. Cash. Five grand."

He looked at me for a long moment, then shook his head and reached down between his legs.

"*Hey*. Whoa!" I shoved the nine a little closer to his face.

"Easy, Starke, easy. It's just a floor safe."

"Slow, Shady. Nice and slow. You pull anything other than money out of it and you're dead."

He pulled a wad of hundreds out of the floor safe, rolled his seat closer to the desk, and started to count. Duvon had pulled himself up onto his ass and sat against the wall. Gold was in the opposite corner, sniffling noisily through the blood. His suit and shirt were a mess. I watched as Tree counted out the bills. When he reached fifty, he tapped the edges to make a neat pile, then he handed them over. "You wanna count it?"

I snatched them out of his hand. "Nope. I already did."

I stuffed the wad into my pocket, reached inside my jacket and pulled out a tiny digital recorder, hit rewind, and then flipped the play button.

"I want to know why your boys beat the shit out of my intern."

"You mean the nosy kid, blond, with pimples? He stuck his face where he shouldn't an' he got caught. Henry here...." It was a bit tinny, but it was clear enough.

"You get the picture, Shady? You call the cops, accuse me of robbing you, and I'll hand this to Lieutenant Gazzara. You'll do time for aggravated assault, and so will your crew."

He glared at me across the desk, that same toothy grimace. "Get outta here, Starke, you crazy bastard. An' don't come back. If you do, they'll fish your body out of the Tennessee. Oh yeah, an' that's two I owe you now: one for the cap you put in my arm, and one for the five grand. I'll be collecting them both when you least expect it."

"Any time, Shady. Any time. But you'd better make sure you get it right, because next time it won't be your arm. Stick out your hands."

"What for?" He glared at me through slitted eyes, the hate bubbling just below the surface.

"You know what for. Stick 'em out, or I'll bust you aside the head with the baton."

"Damn you, Starke. You're gonna pay for this." Reluctantly, he offered his hands, wrists together. I looped a cable tie around them and pulled it tight. He yelped at the pain.

"Now then, Shady. Be a good boy. Sit tight 'till I'm gone, and all will be well."

I took one last look at the two bloody mouseketeers—*yeah, that's what I said, mouse*—as I left, closing the door behind me. Back down the passageway, over the whimpering fat guy near the door, out into the weak winter sunshine. It was a lovely day indeed.

All in all, a good job well done.

Ten minutes later, I was back at my office. As I walked in through the front door, Mike looked up at me over his computer screen. I grinned at him and dropped the wad of cash on his desk.

"Here you go, Mike. Compliments of Mr. Tree. Enjoy."

There was a noisy round of clapping and cheers from the crew. I grinned and shook my head. "Any messages?"

"Yes," Jacque said. "Amanda Cole at Channel Seven wants an interview. When can you do it?"

"Interview? What for?"

"Profile, so she said. I think you should do it. It would be good publicity."

"Nope. Not interested. That young lady has not been kind to me in the past."

Jacque was not pleased, but she'd get over it.

15

I was at a loss as to what to do next. I had plenty of questions and not a lot of answers. I mulled it over and decided that it might be time for another visit to the Sorbonne.

Thursday afternoons are usually quite busy downtown, especially around the aquarium. Chattanooga has become a tourist hotspot over the past twenty years or so. Even on a weekday there are a lot of folks around. Fortunately, the Sorbonne doesn't open until four. It was just after three thirty when I arrived outside the rear door.

I pushed the button and waited. Less than a minute later, I heard the bolt being pulled. The lock turned, and the door opened an inch or two. I gave it a push. Benny stepped back a couple of feet, rubbing his nose. He'd been trying to peer out through the gap. Poor Benny.

"Starke! For Pete's sake, what the hell do you want this time?"

"Just to talk."

"Damn you," he grumbled, turning and walking to his

office. "You touch me again, Starke, and I'll file a complaint. I swear it. I've had a gutful of people bustin' in here and knocking me around."

He waddled round the desk and flopped down in the chair. I looked around the filthy office. The bed didn't look any different from the last time, a pile of dirty sheets and blankets. Two cats sprawled in the middle of all. The other cat was lying on the window ledge, licking its ass. It would have been cute had the whole place not been so disgusting. It stank. *Why in God's name don't the inspectors shut this place down?*

I sat down on the steel chair—I don't think it had been moved since the last time I sat on it—and grinned at him. "People, Benny? Not just me then?"

"Hell no. I had Tree's two pimps in here yesterday. Look what they done to me." He hauled his T-shirt out of his pants and dragged it up over his cadaverous, extended belly, exposing several small but decidedly nasty bruises.

"James and Gold? What did they want?"

"They wanted to know about you, Starke. Wanted to know what you're up to. They knew you were in here that night. They wanted to know if I'd talked to you. I told 'em the truth. I said you were asking about the girl, about them. I told 'em I didn't tell you nothin'. Didn't make a damn bit of difference. Duvon punched me in the gut four times with the barrel of that cannon he drags around with 'im. Told me if I talked to you, or anyone else, about them or Tree again, they'd shoot out my kneecaps. Come on, Harry. Give me a break. They find out you're in here again, they'll be back, and they'll put me in a wheelchair. Why don't you just go and leave me the hell alone?"

"I will, Benny, in a minute. First though, I want you to take a look at a couple of photos."

I flipped the screen on my iPhone and brought up a picture of Charlie Maxwell and showed it to him.

"Do you recognize her, Benny?"

He looked the image, hesitated, then said, "No. Never seen her."

"You sure, Benny? She's never been in the bar?"

"Geez, Harry. What is it you don't understand about the word no? I said I ain't seen her, an' I ain't. You think I wouldn't recognize a good-looking piece of ass like that? I don't know her."

I flipped the screen to a photo of Michael Falk. "How about him?"

"Oh yeah. He comes in now and then, mostly on weekends, late. Has a couple o' drinks, makes a buy, then leaves."

"Makes a buy? Cocaine? Crack?"

"Nah, just weed. Enough for a few joints is all. He's a lightweight."

"When did you last see him?"

He thought for a moment, his face screwed up as he concentrated.

"It's been a while. Friday, I think, late. Not last Friday, the one before. He was with a dude."

"James? Gold?"

"Nah. This guy wasn't one of Tree's people. At least I don't think so. White dude. Never seen him before. Tall guy, big, kinda geeky."

"Go on."

"What's to tell? The guy in the picture came in first, 'bout nine thirty, the other guy a few minutes later. They had one drink, talked, and then left together. Couldn't have been in here more'n fifteen minutes at most."

"Has he been back, the second guy?"

"Nope. Never seen him before or since."

"Anything else you can tell me about him?"

"Nope. Except that he was wearing one of those quilted jackets, an' a ball cap."

Now that got my attention. "Benny. This is important. What color was the jacket?"

"Hell. I dunno, dark. I can't remember, Harry. You know how it is in the bar. Low lights, colored an' all, an' I didn't take any notice anyway. It was a Friday night an' we was busy; I was busy. Wasn't interested. Coulda been any color, but it was too dark to tell."

I looked at him, and he looked away. I wasn't going to get anything else out him, but at least I'd gotten something. I got up and handed him one of my cards.

"Okay, Benny. I believe you. If you remember anything else, especially about the second guy, give me a call, will you?"

He looked at the card, flipped it onto the desktop, and said, "Oh yeah, you can be sure I'll do that."

I smiled at the sarcasm. "Don't bother to get up, Benny. I know the way."

"Yeah, and don't come back."

I walked around the block to where I'd left the car. The meter was about out. I sat inside and thought for a moment. *The second guy? Who the hell is he? Not one of Shady's. He doesn't employ whites. One of Harper's? Could it have been Hope? I wonder.*

I hit the starter, then pulled away and headed home. I'd had enough for one day.

16

The following morning I made it into the office at my usual time. Friday is usually when I gather my staff together to review the week's progress. That Friday was no exception, but I had two appointments scheduled and I needed to take care of them first. I was lucky. One cancelled; the other was a local bail bondsman who wanted to hire us to track down a skip. I told him what I charged. He said it was too expensive and tried to stick me for a professional discount. I told him I only worked for professionals and so didn't give discounts. I gave him a name of someone I thought might cut him a deal, and he left unhappy, but what can you do?

We gathered around the table in the conference room and they laid it out for me. The weekly report was all routine, soon dealt with and dismissed. Then it was on to more interesting things.

"Tim, what have you been able to find out about Willard, Maxwell, and Falk?"

"Not much about any of them, as yet. Falk does indeed work for Harper, for almost five years, mostly as his speechwriter, but I have the feeling that there's more to it than that. He was dating Tabitha Willard on and off for more than a year. His financials suck. He has two bank accounts and is overdrawn on both of them. His credit rating is in the toilet. He seems to have gone AWOL. Not been seen for almost a week. That's about it. I'll keep digging. Maybe something will turn up."

I nodded. "And Tabitha?"

"She's an enigma. No visible means of support, other than her allowance from Old Man Willard. No job that I could find."

"Hold on," I said. "I was told by her father, and by Charlie Maxwell, that she was in public relations."

Tim grinned at me across the table. "Whatever that means. I couldn't find any record of any documented employment for more than a year, but get this: she has almost $80,000 in a savings account and another $11,832 in her checking account."

I shook my head. "How?"

"Dunno. She made regular deposits every week, sometimes more than one. If she's in public relations, you have to ask yourself what kind... if you get my drift."

"Hooker." I didn't like to say it, but...

He looked at me and shrugged.

"As to Charlie Maxwell," Tim continued, "you said she was in computers—IT—and she is. She's employed by a local branch of an outfit based in New York. She makes good money, and has a tidy sum in her savings account, a little more than $37,000, which seems to be about right, considering her income. Her credit is good. She has quite a mortgage on her home—$1,820 monthly—but she can afford it.

"As far as I can tell, she keeps herself mostly to herself. She has no boyfriends that I could find, and very few girlfriends either. She works five days a week. Takes vacations twice a year, usually in the Bahamas but not always. She doesn't drink or do drugs—she has no criminal record. She's clean, Harry."

"That's all good, Tim, but keep digging, especially into Willard. I want to know where that money came from."

He nodded.

"Ronnie, Mike. What were you able to come up with on Harper's Foundation?"

"More than I'm ready to say, right now," Ronnie said. "It's complicated. Can you give me a few more days to tie it all together?"

"Yes, but don't take too long. This is taking a lot more time than I thought it would. We still have a lot of questions and not many answers. I don't want to waste any more of Dr. Willard's retainer than I have to." I smiled. "Okay. Good work, people. Keep it up. Jacque. Do you have anything for me?"

She looked at me long and hard. "I think you should seriously consider the request from Amanda Cole at Channel 7."

I shook my head. "I don't like that woman. She wields a hatchet, and she used it on me last time I talked to her. I swore I would never again give her the time of day." Jacque gave me another look. "Okay, okay," I said, "I'll think about it. But not right now."

Amanda Cole? Screw her.

By the time I was done, it was almost noon. It was Friday. I was out of there. Lunch at the club with my father, then home for the afternoon. Maybe I'd go out for the evening. Maybe not. Kate was on duty, so if I did, it would have to be by myself.

17

It was almost midnight. I'd been in bed for more than an hour, but I couldn't sleep. I'd watched TV for a while. Tried to read a book. But nothing worked, not even three fingers of scotch. My mind was in a whirl. Questions, questions, questions, but not a single solid answer. And then the phone rang. Kate.

"Hey, what's up?"

"You'd better get down here, Harry. They're pulling a body out of the river, a young guy, maybe twenty-five. I can't say for sure, but I think it could be Falk."

Shit. "Where are you exactly?"

"Ross's Landing. Close to the Southern Belle. You'll see the lights."

"I'll be there in twenty." I was already climbing into my clothes, hopping around, wrestling with my jeans. I threw the phone down on the bed, crawled into a hoody, and grabbed my M&P9 and my jacket. I was across the river in ten minutes, burning along Amnicola and then Riverfront Parkway. I pulled to a stop just beyond the tapes. Even at that time of night there was a crowd of looky loos straining their necks, gawking, trying to see what was going on.

Kate was waiting for me and, hell, she had Lonnie Guest with her, and he was in plain clothes.

"Evenin', Starke." He grinned at me as I ducked under the tape, which he was good enough to hold up for me. I ignored him, turned to Kate, twitched my head toward the concrete walkway bordering the river. "Down there?"

"Yeah. Come on.".

Guest followed me, still grinning like a damn Cheshire cat. *What's with this guy?"*

"What's with Guest?" I whispered in Kate's ear.

"He made detective," Kate whispered out of the corner of her mouth. "He's my new partner."

"Oh shit," I said out loud, stopping dead in my tracks. Fat Lonnie barged into my back.

"Sorry, Starke. You need to stay out of the way. This is police work, for *police* officers, (he pronounced it 'poe leece,') of which you ain't one."

"Enough, Lonnie. I invited Harry," Kate said, an edge to her voice. "I know you two can't stand each other, but try to be civil, at least while we're on the job. Okay?"

"Your partner?" I mouthed it silently, but Lonnie spotted it.

"Ain't it a pisser?" he said. "Don't ya just hate it?" The douche was grinning from ear to ear.

I simply shook my head. I had to ignore him, somehow.

The body was lying on the concrete walkway surrounded by a pool of water. The ME had not yet arrived, but the crime scene folks were already there and at work.

"Any idea how he died, and when?" I asked.

"Double tap. Two in the head. Looks like he's been

soakin' for several days, maybe even a week," Lonnie replied, before Kate could even open her mouth.

He'd assumed the pose, legs akimbo, hands on his hips, staring at the body like he knew what the hell he was doing, forcing the photographer to squeeze in around him. There wasn't much room between the body and the water.

Double tap? Where does he get that stuff? Been watching too many gangster movies.

"Two in the head?" I asked Kate.

She nodded. "In the forehead, probably a nine, up close. Not a contact wound; maybe six to eight inches. There's stippling around the wound closest to the bridge of his nose. The second was probably done after he was down."

A 9 mm? I thought about Henry Gold's. I hadn't told Kate about my last visit to see Tree. I'm not sure she would have approved. Still, if the ME found 9 mms in there....

"Professional hit?" I asked.

"Oh yeah," Lonnie said, sniffing. "Had to be. Not common in these parts. Mob hit, prob'ly."

I had to walk away. I was trying not to laugh. The man was an idiot.

I wandered a few yards along the riverfront, got ahold of myself, and then strolled back. Lonnie was gone.

"What did you do with him?" I grinned at her.

"Sent him to the car to report in."

"How in the name of all that's holy did he make detective? Better yet, whose dog did you run over to—"

"Oh hell, Harry," she interrupted. "You know the answer to that. It's not what you know, it's who you know. His cousin is ex-mayor, and I didn't have a partner, so...."

"Sorry, Kate. Must be tough."

"Not so much. He's not that bad really, but he doesn't

like you, which means he becomes a total ass whenever you show up. Anyway, it is what it is, and I can live with it. Hell, I have to."

I nodded. She did, and she would.

"Any identification on the body?"

"Nope, but we'll run his prints, whatever. If he's local, we'll figure it out soon enough; it shouldn't be difficult. This isn't New York. Small Town, U.S.A., right?"

"Right." Everybody knows everybody around here, and even in a town of almost 200,000, someone would know him. A photo in the newspaper or on TV would bring them out of the woodwork. We'd have an ID within twenty-four hours.

"It's Falk. I'd bet money on it. Well dressed. Dark gray business suit, white shirt, blue tie, black loafers. He's about the right age, and the timing's right, too. If he's been in the water a week, that would make it Friday evening. Has to be, he's still dressed in his work clothes, and Benny said he saw him in the Sorbonne that Friday night with a guy he'd never seen before. If it had been the weekend, he would probably have been dressed in jeans and a tee."

"You could be right. We'll know more when we get the autopsy report... ah, here's Doc Sheddon now."

I looked off into the flashing lights. A small man, overweight, bald head, carrying a large black case was hurrying toward us.

"Good evening, Lieutenant. How's it hanging, Harry? Whew. Why do these things always happen late at night?" he said to nobody in particular. He dropped down beside the body, opened his case, snapped on a pair of latex gloves, and went about his business. It took him less than five minutes before he stood and waved for the gurney.

"Not much to be done here. He's been in the water five to seven days. Cause of death? Well, you can see that for yourself. You need this one in a hurry, I suppose," he said, looking at Kate. "I'll get on it tomorrow. Probably won't be until after lunch. I'll see you then, Lieutenant. You can attend, too, Harry, if you like."

"Maybe. Thanks, Doc."

He nodded, and then hurried away through the lights.

"I have to be there, Harry, and I would imagine that Lonnie will want to be there, too, being a new detective and all."

"Good luck with that," I said with a grin. "I'll pass. You can give me a call when you know more. I'm going home. I need some sleep."

"You surely do, Harry. This is a murder case now. My case. If it is Falk, it's connected, and I'll be going to see Harper, probably early Monday morning. You want to join me?"

"Oh yes."

"Okay. Sleep tight. I'll head out myself in a minute or two."

I left her there, watching them load the body onto the gurney. I shuddered. There's something so terribly final about those black vinyl body bags.

18

It was just after seven when I awoke the following morning. I thought for a moment about Falk, and then pushed it to the back of my mind. Although I don't have to go into the office on weekends, I usually did, but not that weekend. I got out of bed, went to the kitchen, made myself a cup of Dark Italian roast, then went back to bed to drink it. It was still quite dark outside, but the view over the river was a joy to behold. It's times like these when I remember why I bought the place. In the distance, I could see the lights moving across the Thrasher Bridge. I lay back on the pillows, closed my eyes, and sipped my coffee. Life wasn't all bad.

I enjoy those quiet moments; they are few and far between, and this one didn't last for long. The phone rang, and I jumped like a scalded cat.

Damn it, this had better be good.

"Hello?"

I had no idea who was calling, and I didn't give a damn.

"Mr. Starke?"

"That's me."

"Mr. Starke. This is Charlie Maxwell. I wondered if I could talk to you. I think I have a problem."

I sighed. *What the hell could she want at this time on a Saturday morning?*

"Tell me."

"Umm, I'd rather tell you in person. I'm... well. I'm... frightened."

"Frightened?" I sat up in bed. "Why?"

"I think I'm being followed, stalked."

That got my attention.

"Stay right where you are. Don't open the door to anyone but me. I'll be there as quick as I can. Where are you?"

"I live on Enclave Bay Drive, just off Carter Drive. Do you know it?"

"I do."

She gave me the address, and I jumped out of bed and headed for the bathroom. I gulped down the last of my coffee, showered, tidied up the fuzz on my face, and headed out.

The Enclave is an upscale subdivision on the north shore of the river, less than five miles from where I live. The drive took about ten minutes.

I found her house, a smallish Cape Cod affair that backed onto the river. Not one of the most expensive homes in the neighborhood, but high dollar just the same.

I parked the car in front of the house, walked up the three steps, and reached for the bell. The door opened before I could push the button.

She'd been waiting for me.

I took one look at her and almost took a step backward.

I'd thought she was a beauty the first time I met her, but now —just, wow.

She was almost as tall as me even barefoot, and I'm six-two. Her hair was piled on top of her head in a tangled heap that, at first glance, looked unkempt, but it wasn't, which only added to her tawny, cat-like look. She was dressed, if you could call it that, in a white T-shirt that just about covered her backside. It had the words, 'I'm Sleepy,' emblazoned across the front. *Whew. She doesn't look sleepy to me.*

Her legs would have made a weaker man drool.

"Thank you for coming, Harry. Get back, Buster. Let the man come in." She was talking to a feisty little West Highland white terrier that was looking for attention. "Give me a minute. I'll put him outside."

She turned and walked in front of me, and I followed her inside. *Yep, that shirt barely covers her ass.*

I looked around the living room. "Nice place," I said when she returned.

"Thank you."

"I have to wonder, Charlie. How can you afford it?"

She laughed, a husky, sexy laugh. "You're not the first to ask that question. The truth is, I got lucky. It was a foreclosure. I bought it cheap, and I make good money. I'm good at what I do. Now, come on into the kitchen. Please, sit down." She waved her hand in the direction of a group of tall stools at the breakfast bar. "How about some coffee?"

I nodded, sat, and watched, hypnotized, as she went about making it. She poured two cups, walked around the bar, put them down on the marble surface, pulled back one of the stools, hitched up the T-shirt, and sat down, gifting me with a flash of white underwear. I felt like I'd been body-slammed, and she knew it, but there was more yet to come.

She had seated herself in front of me, on the same side of the breakfast bar. She had one foot on the floor, the other on the rail of the stool. The effect was heart-stopping. I was treated to a tantalizing and continuous view of... and I couldn't take my eyes off it. She leaned forward, pushing one of the cups toward me and then picking up the other. Her legs were everywhere. She put the cup to her lips and breathed gently over the rim, and was still gazing up at me from beneath lowered eyelids when she took a sip. It was some performance. Oh, she was good.

I managed to drag my eyes away from the vision between her legs to take a sip of my own coffee. I looked her in the eye and said, "Nice." I was talking about the coffee, but I could tell by the way she smiled that she thought I was talking about something else.

"So, you wanted to see me," I said. Hell, I had to get my mind working again.

"Yes. I think I'm being stalked."

"So you said on the phone. Tell me about it."

"Well, it started when I left the Read House, after I met you. I'd left my car in that multi-story parking lot just down the road from the coffee shop. I noticed him as soon as I walked outside. He was on the far side of the street, in a doorway. I didn't think anything of it at the time; it was cold and I supposed he was sheltering from the wind."

I nodded. "What did he look like? Did he follow you?"

"No, he didn't follow me; at least I don't think so. He was tall, quite well built—white, I think. He was wearing a heavy jacket and a ball cap. It was hard to tell. I've seen him two more times since. I saw him again, the next day, in the morning, at the gym... I work out most days."

I had no doubt that she did, but the look she gave me as

she said it was as much a message as it was information. I did my best to ignore it.

"Where did you see him the third time? How do you know it was him?"

"Well, it looked like the same man. It was yesterday, which is why I called you. I went shopping. I needed some new clothes. He was leaning against the wall, a couple of doors down from the clothing store."

"Which store? Where?"

"Angelique. On McCallie."

"I put my cup down and looked at her. "Angelique? In the new strip mall?"

"Yes. Do you know it?"

"I do. Tell me how he was dressed."

"The same as before: dark jeans and one of those puffy, quilted coats, dark red or maybe maroon, and a Braves ball cap."

I nodded. It sounded like it might be the same guy who was with Falk in the Sorbonne.

"You sure he was white?"

She nodded. "Pretty sure, but... well I guess he could have been black. He had his hands in his pockets, and the cap was pulled down over his eyes."

"What about his hair?"

"It was under the cap."

It could be the same guy, but it could also be Duvon James. If it was, he was probably following me. The Read House, the mall. Duvon works out of the mall. He had every reason to be there. But, if not.... Maybe it was just coincidence, but that's too much of a coincidence.

"And you saw him at the gym, too?" I tilted my head sideways as I looked at her.

"Yes, at the gym."

She shifted, dropped the one leg on the rail to the floor and lifted the other up to take its place.

Oh my God. Oh my God.

"And the gym is...?" I already knew the answer.

"It's a couple of doors away from Angelique. It's brand new and they have lots of good help, trainers, and such."

It was time to put her at ease.

"Charlie, I don't think you have anything to worry about. I think I may know who the man is and what he was doing at the mall. If I'm right, his name is Duvon James, and he works there, in the office at the end of the block."

"Oh!" She seemed disappointed. "But what was he doing at the Read House?"

"I had a run in with his boss that morning. It was a bit... intense. I think it was me he was following."

"Well," she said. "That makes me feel a whole lot better. Thank you."

It didn't make me feel better. I wasn't absolutely sure I had it figured right, and I hated to admit that even to myself. If it wasn't Duvon, who the hell was it? I looked at her. She looked at me.

"You sure it was the same man you saw all three times?" I asked.

She just shrugged.

"Call me if you see him again, and I'll look into it. In the meantime, take care."

I stood and put my cup down on the counter. I was about to leave, but... As I turned, she slid off the stool, took a step toward me, pressed herself against me, put her arms around my neck, and planted her lips squarely on mine. I was so taken aback, I let it happen. At least that's what I told myself later.

I don't think I'll ever forget that kiss. It was so sudden, so complete. Her lips were moist, parted slightly. I have no idea how long it lasted, but I enjoyed every long, lingering second.

I pushed her gently away. She looked up at me, her mouth still slightly parted, her eyes hooded. I stepped back, and her arms dropped away.

"Not a good idea, Charlie."

"Why not? Are you married? Is there a girlfriend?"

I nodded. "Something like that, but that isn't it. It's unethical."

She smiled. "So. You do like me, then."

I grinned at her. "What's not to like? Sorry, Charlie. I need to go. I have another appointment."

She sighed, walked through the living room toward the door—there was that backside again—and opened the door. "Will I see you again?" she asked.

"I'm sure you will." *But not the way you want.* I paused in the doorway. "Oh, by the way. Tabitha's boyfriend, Michael Falk. He's dead. Murdered."

I watched her face carefully. Her eyes opened wide; so did her mouth.

"What? How?" No doubt about it. She was horrified.

"I don't know anything yet, but when I do, I'll let you know. Oh, and I'm sure the police will want to talk to you."

I left her standing there, staring after me. She was pale. Her eyes were watering. *Not an act. If it is, she's damned good.*

I got back into my car, turned on the radio, and sat there with my head spinning. I could still taste her, feel her, and that view... I'd never forget it. There was just something about her. There was also something else, but I just couldn't figure it out.

I started the car and drove north, out of the Enclave, hit the Bluetooth, and called Kate. I needed to get back to reality.

"Hey, what's up?"

"Let's do breakfast. I need to talk to you."

"Okay. Where? When?"

"How about the IHOP on Brainerd in say," I glanced at the clock on the dash, "thirty minutes?"

"Make it an hour. I just got back from the gym and I need to clean up."

"Not you, too," I muttered.

"What's that? I didn't hear you."

"Nothing. I'll tell you all about it over breakfast, okay?"

She said that it was, and I headed across town. I made a stop at the liquor store on the way, grabbed a couple of bottles of red and a large bottle of Bombay Sapphire—my stock of gin was almost out—and I headed east. And then it hit me. I'd been so preoccupied with Charlie Maxwell that I'd forgotten to ask her if I could take a look at Tabitha's room. *Too late now. I sure as hell am not going back there today. Another time... maybe.*

I waited in the parking lot until Kate arrived. When she did, it was as if a breath of fresh air had wafted in off the river. She was wearing black woolen hose, a short dark red skirt, and a black roll-neck sweater. Her hair was set in a ponytail on the left side of her head; it covered her ear and part of her cheek. As always, she looked stunning. I heaved a sigh, stepped out of the car, and took her hand. At that moment, I think I was as happy as I had ever been.

We sat opposite each other in a quiet booth in a corner of the restaurant and sipped coffee while we waited for our order to arrive. She looked at me, her eyebrows raised in a silent question.

I took a deep breath, looked her in the eye, and said, "I had a call from Charlotte Maxwell this morning," I said, and then hesitated.

"Go on."

"She was frightened. Said she wanted to see me. Said she thought she was being stalked... So I went."

"Okay."

"Kate, she was the next best thing to naked. All she was wearing was a T-shirt and panties."

"Panties? How do you know?"

"I could see them. I should have turned right around and left, but I didn't. Knowing what I know, I figured she might well have someone after her. Turns out though, there wasn't, at least I don't think so. I think the guy she saw was following me, but that's not what I want to talk to you about."

She leaned both elbows on the table, rested her chin on her hands, and stared at me; there was the makings of a smile on her lips.

"Go on."

I looked at her for a long moment. "She kissed me."

"She kissed you?" There was no emotion in the question, just three quiet words.

I nodded. "Yeah, she kissed me."

"And?"

"And, and, and, nothing." I was stuttering. "That was it. I pushed her away and I got outta there, fast."

"So, no harm done then."

I heaved an inward sigh of relief, but then...

She looked at me for a moment, a slight smirk on her face, then said, "And did you enjoy it?"

I was about to say, "Not only no, but hell no." But I didn't. I looked down at the table, then back at her, then nodded. "I did."

"Right answer, Harry. Like I said, no harm done. Only a complete idiot would claim they didn't enjoy being kissed by a beautiful woman. Just don't let it happen again."

And that was it. It wasn't a threat. She well knew my weaknesses, and she tolerated them, to a point. Anyway, she said no more about it, and I knew better than to bring it up again.

She left around eleven. Said she needed to go into the office. I went to mine. I spent a few hours browsing through some records, but my heart wasn't in it. I couldn't get my mind off Charlie Maxwell. Nope, it wasn't what you're thinking. There was something about that girl. Something wasn't quite gelling, as they say. Maybe it would come to me. Then again, maybe it wouldn't.

I headed home about four. I didn't plan on seeing Kate that evening, since she was on call, but I did give Dad a call and suggested he buy me dinner.

He said he would, so I showered and put on some decent clothes, minus the M&P9, and headed out again. He was already there, and already a little the worse for wear, it looked like. But Anyway, I met him at six and we sat down together.

Now, there's one thing you have to understand about my father: he's a showman, larger than life. He's as fit and toned as I am and an inch taller, with silver hair, not unlike like

Donald Trump's. He was wearing a black golf shirt, accented by a gold chain necklace that would choke a horse, black slacks, and a pair of black loafers. He wears his wealth well, does my old dad.

He ordered a T-bone steak with all the trimmings, and ate it all. I had a chicken Caesar salad and left most of it. I wasn't that hungry.

Afterward, we sat in the lounge and talked. He wasn't, as I'd thought, under the influence, not even a little bit.

"So, Harry. What's going on?"

I shook my head. "Damned if I know. I went to see Harper on Thursday. I gave him your check. Stirred his pot a little. He was... how shall I put it? He was quietly evasive. I got the distinct impression he thought I might be recording the conversation. I wasn't, but I'm damned sure *he* was. How well do you know him, Dad?"

"Not well at all. I've met him a couple of times socially, and I know about his good works. I've just never have moved in the same circles of power. He's very wealthy, and there's been some talk about influence peddling, voter fraud, among other things, but it's just talk, as far as I know. Why are you so interested in him?"

"It's something Kate asked me to do, but now.... Well, I get the feeling there's something very nasty going on, and that he might be involved."

I reached into my pocket for the pendant. "Have you ever seen anything like this before?"

He looked at it, squinted, and turned it over in his hand. "Maybe... I think, maybe I might have seen something like it before. One of the lady members here, perhaps, but I don't know what it is. Where did you get it?"

"That's three, then, if you're right. Tabitha Willard was

wearing this one when she jumped off the bridge. I have no idea what it is, either, but Harper was wearing a ring with the same motif."

He raised his eyebrows at that.

"It must mean something," I said. "They can't just be decorative. Can they?"

He shook his head and handed the pendant back to me. "I don't know. I'll keep a lookout for it. Maybe I'll run across her again, the lady member."

"Thanks. If you spot it, let me know who it is. Don't worry. I'll be discreet. In the meantime, I'm having Tim look into it. I'm also having Ronnie look into the Harper Foundation."

He nodded. "How about the Willard girl? Have you found anything?"

"Oh, there's something there all right. They dragged her boyfriend's body out of the river late last night. Well, we think it was him. Guy named Falk, Michael Falk. He was one of Harper's speechwriters. He was murdered. Shot. Two in the head. So now we have Tabitha Willard connected through Falk to Harper, and through Stimpy and Ren to Lester Tree. Harper's involved in something. I know he is. I'm going to get him, Dad. Bring him down, and Tree along with him."

"Stimpy and Ren?"

I smiled. "Two very nasty types I saw arguing with Tabitha in the Sorbonne the night she died. Their names are Duvon James and Henry Gold; they work for Tree."

"I see," he said, with a wry smile. "You need to be careful, son."

"Count on it."

I looked at the pendant. *So now there are three. Hmmm.*

I slipped it back into my pocket, spent another half hour making small talk with my father, then said goodbye, and headed home.

I hadn't even left the country club parking lot when I noticed a car pull out behind me. I couldn't see the make or model—it was too dark—but I could see it was either black or dark blue. I let it follow me for about a mile, then made a sharp left onto Altamont, killed the lights, and floored it all the way to Memorial. Then I hit the brakes and pulled off to the side of the road. Seconds later, a late-model BMW two-door hurtled past, heading toward Dayton Boulevard. I grinned. I'd seen that car before, parked at the rear of Shady Tree's office. *Good evening, Stimpy and Ren.*

I pulled a U-turn and drove quietly back home. The Beemer was parked 100 yards or so down the road from my condo. I drove slowly past it. I couldn't see in—the windows were tinted almost black—but I slowed, rolled my window down, grinned out at whoever it was, waved, made a U-turn and returned to my home. I hit the garage door opener, drove inside, closed the door, and went into the kitchen and looked out of the window. They were still there.

They were still there when I went to bed, so I retrieved the nine from the safe, set the alarm, and was soon lost in a whirl of thoughts and fantasy.

19

As always, I was awake early the next morning, Sunday. The first thing I did was go to the kitchen window. The Beemer was gone. Not a big deal. I didn't know for sure, but I was pretty certain it belonged to Shady's two goons, or even Shady himself, though why he would get down and dirty and follow me himself made no sense. No, it was Duvon and Henry.

Rarely do I do anything work related on Sundays, and I was determined that this Sunday would be no different from any other. So I got up, straightened the bed—no housekeeper today—showered, made some coffee, toast, scrambled eggs with cheese, and settled down to read the paper.

At about eleven o'clock, I called Kate and asked her to lunch, then went to pick her up.

"Where d'you want to eat?"

She screwed up her face. "I dunno. You pick."

I nodded. "Somewhere in the Art District, I think. I'd like to take a quick walk first, if that's okay."

"Sure. Where?"

"I'd like to take another look at the bridge."

"Walnut Street. Fine. Let's go."

I slipped the car into gear and headed north to I-24. We arrived in the downtown area just after noon and parked off Walnut Street. From there it was a walk of a few hundred yards to the bridge. The day was sunny, but chilly. Even so, the walkers were out in force, and traffic on the bridge was heavy.

We strolled to the place where Tabitha Willard had taken her dive into eternity and sat down on the same bench we'd occupied the night she killed herself.

We sat and talked for a moment, then I left Kate on the bench and wandered over to the rail. It all came flooding back. I could hear her heels clicking on the pavement, see the wild looks she cast back over her shoulder, and finally those huge, scared eyes that bored into mine, and then... I shook the images out of my head and returned to the bench.

"Come on, let's walk." I took her hand, and we walked across the bridge to the north side of the river, past Coolidge Park and out onto River Street. There were some nice places to eat there, but nothing I fancied.

We strolled back over the bridge, onto Walnut. The walk had been a waste of time. I'd been hoping that a return to the scene might jog my memory, but it hadn't. It looked very different in daylight, with people churning around everywhere.

We made our way slowly up to the Bluff View Art District. It was almost one o'clock by then, and I was getting hungry.

"Tony's okay?"

She looked sideways at me and nodded.

We went inside. Lunchtime is always busy up there,

especially on weekends. We had to wait for a table, but not for long. After only ten minutes or so, a couple by the window got up and walked to the register. We dropped into their seats.

I had the chicken parmesan. Kate had a Sicilian salad. As always, the food was excellent. Kate, however, was in a somewhat pensive mood.

"Harry, I'm going to see Harper tomorrow morning. You're welcome to come with me, if you want."

"Sure, but do you think it's a good idea to go without a positive I.D? We still don't know if it's Falk or not."

"Oh, it's him all right. I found a photo of him on Harper's website. He was with a bunch of other people, but it was him. I have the itch, Harry, and I need to scratch it. I'd go today if I could, but... well, he is a congressman and it is Sunday. It can wait until tomorrow. So you'll come with me?"

"Yup. You want me to pick you up? What time? Where?"

"Pick me up on Amnicola, outside the police department. As early as you like. I'd like to get to him before he has time to settle in, get comfortable."

"Sounds good. I'll be in the lot out front at eight thirty. What do you want to do the rest of today? You want me to drop you off at home, or what?"

"No. Let's go to your place. We can have a nice quiet afternoon, I'll make us something nice for dinner, and then... well, we'll see."

I grinned at her. "We can do that."

20

I picked Kate up at the police department just before eight thirty Monday morning, and we headed right on over to Harper's offices.

"Where's your boy?" I asked, referring to her new partner, Lonnie Guest.

"Left him at his desk. He wasn't happy, but what the hell."

We headed for the elevator, and she punched the button for the top floor. I watched her as we rode on up. Kate is really two people: one is the nice girl with the bright smile and easygoing attitude everyone loves, and then there's the tough, intimidating no nonsense cop that nobody dares to fool with. I watched her attitude change from one to the other as we rode the elevator. By the time we reached the top floor, the transformation was complete.

The elevator doors opened and, without a glance in my direction, she strode out into the corridor. She opened Harper's outer office door and strode in, badge in hand.

"I'm here to see Congressman Harper," she told the young man behind the reception desk.

"Is there something I can help you with? I'm afraid he's busy."

"Me too." She looked at me. I pointed to Harper's inner office door. She walked past the receptionist, opened it, and strode inside.

"What the hell?"

"Congressman Harper. I am Lieutenant Catherine Gazzara." She held out her badge. "I need a moment of your time. I have some questions about Michael Falk. I believe he's an employee of yours."

"He is, but what the hell is Starke doing here? He's not a police officer."

"He is here at my invitation, as a consultant, and with the full knowledge of my superiors. If you have any objections, you may take it up with them. Do you need the number?"

He shook his head, looking around her at the man seated on the far side of the room, opposite the window, at a desk that was far too small for him. "Take notes, Jackson."

Hope took a small digital recorder from his desk drawer, turned it on, and then swiveled his chair around to face us.

"Take a seat, Lieutenant. You, too, Starke," Harper said.

We sat. He looked across his desk at us, switching his gaze from Kate to me and back again.

"So, what about Falk? What's he been up to?"

"He's dead. That's what he's been up to," Kate said, looking at him steadily.

He sat back in his chair and stared at her. He didn't even twitch an eyelid.

No reaction. He already knew.

"Dead? How? An accident? What?"

"Murder, Congressman. He was murdered. Shot twice in the head. We took him out of the river at Ross's Landing late Friday night."

"The hell you say. All right. What does that have to do with me? He worked here, that's all. I let him go last Friday, more than a week ago. Jackson here," he twitched his head in the other man's direction, "escorted him off the property, and I haven't seen him since."

"So you fired him. What for?"

"He was one of my speechwriters, but he thought he knew what I wanted to say better than I did. He wouldn't listen to me so I let him go. No big deal."

I watched him carefully as he said it. It rang true, but... *Why have him escorted off the property for such a minor infraction?*

"You fired him for bad writing?" Kate asked. "That's a bit harsh, don't you think?"

"I fire people for all sorts of reasons, Lieutenant. I can't abide inefficiency, nor a lack of willingness to learn or take direction. Falk was all of that."

This interview was going nowhere fast. Harper wasn't giving her an inch.

"What about his office? His computer? Can we take a look?"

"His office has been reallocated, and his computer has been recycled. It was an older laptop and it needed to be replaced. I have no idea what happened to it. Anything else, Lieutenant?"

"When was the last time you saw him?"

"That Friday morning when I let him go. I haven't seen hide nor hair of him since."

"How about your staff? What about him?" She nodded in Jackson's direction. He opened his mouth to speak, but Harper beat him to it.

"He hasn't seen him either, and the only permanent staff I have here is Jackson and my receptionist, and he never leaves this office. Now, if there's nothing else..."

I decided it was time for me to jump in.

"I have something," I said smoothly. "When I left this office the other day, you had me followed. Why?"

Harper stared at me, unblinking; so did Hope.

"Starke, you have a vivid imagination. No one from this office followed you."

"That's a typical politician's answer. I didn't say it was someone from this office. I said you had me followed. Care to try again?"

Hope started to rise. So did I. Kate put a hand on my arm. Harper raised his hand and gestured for Hope to sit, which he did, reluctantly. Very wise of him.

"Lieutenant, I suggest you leave my office and take your half-wit side kick with you, right now. I am a United States Congressman, and I don't have to put up with your crap. You can be sure that I'll call the mayor and lodge an official complaint about your conduct—yours and your amateur G-man's. Now get out of here, and don't come back, either of you."

We both rose to our feet. "Oh I'll be back, Congressman. You can bet on it." She wasn't the least bit intimidated by him. "In the meantime, if you think of anything that might be helpful, especially about Michael Falk, I'd appreciate a call. Here's my card."

She offered it to him, but he didn't lift so much as finger. She placed it in front of him on the desk, and we left.

I could feel his stare burning a hole in the center of my back.

"Whew." She heaved a big sigh as walked toward the elevator. "Nice one, Harry. You sure know how to get under someone's skin. We were not there to antagonize him, just to feel him out."

"We did that, Kate. They already knew Falk was dead; you *know* that. You could tell by their reaction, or rather the lack of it. Not much from Harper, and none at all from Hope, which tells me that he at least must have known that Falk was dead. The media hasn't gotten hold of it yet, have they?"

She shook her head.

"Okay then. So how *could* they have known? I guarantee it was that son of a bitch Hope that killed him. But why? Fire him? Yes, I can see why he might do that, but kill him? He must have gotten himself into something... but what?"

Kate pushed the down button and we waited.

"I don't know," she said. "But you're right; neither one of them seemed surprised."

"Precisely. We know Falk must have worked closely with Harper. Had to have. He was his speechwriter, for God's sake. You'd think there'd be some reaction or surprise, at least some small sign of shock when they heard."

"Stranger things, Harry. Stranger things."

"By the way," I said as we entered the elevator. "Did you notice Harper's ring?"

"I did. It's a smaller version of the pendant, right?"

"Yup. I noticed it the first time I interviewed him, but I didn't mention it then because I wanted Tim to see if he could find out anything about it. He hasn't so far, but here's the thing. I had dinner with Dad last night, at the country club. I showed him the pendant. He thinks he might have seen it before, on one of the lady members. He couldn't remember who it was, but he said he'd try to find out. That's three of them. It can't be a coincidence. There has to be a connection. We need to find out what it is. I asked Harper about his ring when I was here the other day. He showed it to me. Said it was a gift from a friend, and that he had no idea what it meant."

"So what's your plan?

"I don't have one yet. I need to go back to the office. There's a couple of things I need to do. After that, I'll get some lunch. You want to join me?"

"Hmm. Me, too, go to the office, that is, so I can't."

"Okay. I'll drop you off, then."

It was less than an hour later that Kate called. I took it my office.

"What do you know, Harry? I'd barely walked in the door when I was called in to see the Chief. Harper didn't waste any time. He'd called the mayor, and the mayor called Johnston. I got my ass chewed and I've been warned off. I have to stay away from Harper, and I was told to tell you to stay away from him, too. I can't go near him now unless I have probable cause."

"But it's a murder investigation. How're you supposed to conduct it if you can't question Falk's employer and his staff?"

"I can't, unless I have a good reason, and even then I have to clear it with Johnson first."

"Now you know why I quit the Job. Too much damned

bureaucracy. Too many rules. Well, I don't have any rules. I can do as I please. As far as I'm concerned, Harper is just another bad guy, and I'm going after him."

"How did I know that? Be careful, Harry. Harper's a very powerful man, and he won't hesitate to cut you down, if he can. You may not have to follow the same rules I do, but they can pull your license any time they want." *That might be tougher than you think, Kate.*

She was right, of course, but what the hell. I have powerful friends, too, including a Federal judge.

"I'll be careful."

"Good. I'll help any way I can, but you *must* keep me in the loop. Don't let me get sideswiped. You know what I mean, right?"

"I do. Don't worry. I have your back."

"One more thing, I have the autopsy results on Falk. The cause of death was two in the head: nine millimeter. One was mashed all to hell when it hit the skull; the other has some damage, but there are clear lands and grooves. If we can find the weapon, we should be able to make a match."

"Anything on the time of death?"

"Not much more than we had," she said. "Midnight, Friday night, the sixteenth, give or take eight hours. That puts it roughly between four in the afternoon and eight in the morning on Saturday. Dressed as he was, I'd put it earlier rather than later. You said he was in the Sorbonne at nine-thirty, so say between then and midnight, but it's just a guess."

"Yeah, maybe. It's something to think about."

"All right. Talk to you later."

I hung up the phone, sat back in my chair, and stared up at the ceiling.

Okay, so Falk is murdered and tossed into the river on Friday evening between nine-thirty and midnight. His ex-girlfriend is scared out of her brains and throws herself off the bridge two days later. Why was she so scared? Did she know Falk was dead? Duvon and Henry? Had to be. But why? Nasty pair of... What were they after? Had to be something for Shady... or Harper. Nope, Harper wouldn't be seen dead around those two... but, if Shady works for Harper... And who the hell killed Falk, and why? Hmmm. Harper, Hope, Shady, Stimpy and Ren. And then there's this.

I fished in my pocket for the pendant. Turned it over and over in my fingers. *What are you all about?*

I picked up my phone, dialed, and waited. He picked up on the second ring.

"Dad, it's me. Any word on who was wearing the pendant?"

"No, Harry. I'm at the club now, for lunch. I'll see what I can find. If I come up with anything, I'll call you back."

Click.

I dialed again. "Kate. Can you go and check out the gym? Today, if possible. Maybe you should join, work out, and the two clothing stores. I can't do it. Tree and his crew know me."

"Okay. It's about lunchtime. I'll head over there now."

"Great. And don't make any plans for tomorrow night. We're going to dinner, at La Maison Ducat. Call me if you find anything. Later. Bye."

I hung up.

More. I need to know more.

I was just about to leave the office to get some lunch when my cell phone rang.

"Harry, it's me." It was my father. "I found her. She's the wife of one of the members. Can you come over? I'll introduce you."

"Good timing. I was just heading out to lunch. I'll be there in twenty."

When I walked into the club lounge, I spotted them sitting at a table in one of the bay windows overlooking the ninth green. She was quite something, a little older than I'd expected. Why I was expecting someone younger I had no idea, but I was. Anyway, from the way she was dressed, she'd obviously been playing tennis. I had the idea she might be quite tall, although it was hard to tell, sitting at the table as she was. I could tell she was fit: her calf muscles were sharply defined, and so were her arms. Her breasts were a little on the small side, but also clearly defined. Her blond hair was short, sculpted to the nape of her neck. I figured she must be in her mid to late forties, but she didn't look more than thirty-five. This was one classy lady.

I approached the table. My father rose, but she remained seated.

"Ah, Harry. There you are. This is Olivia Hansen. Olivia, this is my son, Harry."

"Hello, Harry." The voice suited her looks, breathy, mid-toned. "It's nice to meet you. Please, sit down."

"It's nice to meet you, too, Mrs. Hansen."

"Oh please, call me Olivia."

I nodded, smiled, and sat down opposite her; my father was between us with his back to the window, facing the room.

"So, Harry. You look fit. Sports?" She was making small talk. *Oh my... there it is.*

Hanging from a thin gold chain around her neck, was the twin of the pendant I had in my pocket. For a moment, I was speechless.

"What's the matter?" She leaned forward as she said it. "You look like you've seen a ghost."

I shook my head. "Nothing, really. I just had a funny thought, that's all."

"Oh please, share it with us."

"Nah, it wasn't that funny, and probably not appropriate." I could have bitten my tongue off. *What a damned stupid thing to say.*

"Not appropriate. That sounds intriguing." And the look she gave me as she said it was intriguing, too. She tilted her head slightly to one side, lowered her chin slightly, and looked up at me through her eyelashes.

The drinks waiter came and took our order. Dad had a gin and tonic, Olivia had a Mimosa, and I had a Blue Moon beer, no orange slice.

We sat for several moments, making small talk. I couldn't take my eyes off her pendant. Then I looked at my father and made a tiny gesture with my eyes; he got the message.

"I wonder if I could leave you alone for a moment or two," he said as he rose from his seat. "I'm in the middle of an important case, and I need to make a couple of calls. It shouldn't take too long. Do you mind?"

Good old dad. Ever the diplomat. We both shook our heads and watched him walk through the lounge and out into the foyer.

"So, Harry. What is it you do for a living? Something...

manual, I would imagine, from the look of you." It was said with a slight smile, but I wasn't quite sure how to take it.

"Actually, Mrs. Hansen—Olivia. I'm a private investigator."

"Oh how *interesting*." Yes, she was a class act. She leaned forward, elbows on the table, her chin rested on top of her hands. "I've never met one before, a private eye? Or is it a private *dick?*"

I had my drink up to my mouth, and I almost choked on it. It wasn't the first time I'd heard that worn out old tag, but this lady was a trip. I put the drink down, sat back in my chair, and laughed. Really laughed—head thrown back, mouth open—and so did she, evidently very pleased with herself.

And that set the tone for the rest of the conversation.

"Tell me, Harry, are you married?"

"No. Are you?"

"Of course. Who around here isn't? My husband is in transportation. Hansen Trucking. Have you heard of it?"

Who the hell hasn't? Their trucks are everywhere.

"Of course. Hansen is a big outfit."

"One of the biggest. It pays for my rather... shall we say, extravagant lifestyle."

Okay, time to take the plunge. "Olivia, I noticed your pendant. It's rather unusual."

"It is, isn't it?"

There was a twinkle in her eye as she said it, but that's all she said.

"Yes. I have one just like it."

That got her attention.

"You *do?*"

How can I put it? The way she said it was a question, but

also a statement, and the question was, I had a feeling, double-barreled: two questions in one.

I nodded and fished it out of my pocket and held it up for her to see.

"May I see it?" She held out her hand. I gave it to her.

She turned it over in her fingers, rotated it, with a somewhat enigmatic smile on her lips.

"So you do. Why aren't you wearing it?" She handed it back to me, leaned back in her chair, and smiled at me. No, it was more than a smile. *An invitation, perhaps?*

"I went swimming this morning, at the 'Y.'' Where the hell did that come from? I hadn't been swimming in years. "I took it off and just haven't put it back on again."

She had a funny sort of look on her face, as if she was expecting something. I was at a loss. I didn't want to ask questions. I was trying like hell not to give the game away. I didn't want her to know that I didn't know what the pendant was, so I waited, smiling at her. She continued to smile at me. I slipped the pendant back into my pocket, reached for my beer, and sipped on it, looking at her over the rim of the glass as I did so.

After a moment of silence between us, she reached into her purse and took out a pen and a business card. After she'd written something on the back, she slid it across the table, then rose to her feet, turned and walked away without a word. I gazed after her. There's something alluring about a shapely woman in tennis strip, and this one was no exception. She walked quickly, her hips rolling as she went; yes, alluring.

I looked down at the card, at what she'd written. I was stunned. It was an address: *19 Alderney Gardens, Apt 9. Five o'clock. Don't be late.*

I looked up, but she was gone. My father was walking back into the room, looking back over his shoulder as he came toward me.

"Did you learn anything?" He sat down, a half-smile on his face.

"Oh yeah, but what the hell it all meant, I haven't a clue. What do you know about her, Dad?"

"Not a whole lot. I've met her once or twice before. She's married, though she's rarely here with her husband. Nice sort, Hansen. Wealthy, very wealthy. She plays a lot of tennis. Not sure if it's because she likes the game or the instructors. She's here quite often. Lots of friends. All upscale. No scandal that I know of. That's about it."

I looked at my watch. It was already close to two o'clock, and I needed a shower and a change of clothes.

I got up from the table. "Gotta go, Dad. Places to go. People to see. Later, okay?"

He nodded. "Good luck, son." He said it with a knowing smile.

I nodded and left him there, staring after me.

21

Alderney Gardens is a small gated community just off Brainerd Road. I gave the gate guard my name, and he opened the gates. It was five after five when I parked the car outside number nine, a one-story condo.

"You're late," she said once she'd opened the door. "I told you not to be late." She was smiling.

"Five minutes." I grinned back at her. "Just five minutes."

She had changed, too. She was wearing a loose white cotton dress, no shoes, and not much else. I could see the outline of her body in the backlight of the window behind her.

"Well," she said as she stepped aside for me to enter, "don't you look nice? That's so much better than the nasty black outfit you were wearing."

I wasn't wearing a whole lot myself: tan slacks, a blue golf shirt, loafers with no socks.

We entered what I assumed was the living room. It was

nicely furnished but not out of the ordinary, with a large picture window that overlooked the gardens.

"This is nice," she said, as she turned to face me.

She put her hands on my forearms, came up onto her toes, and kissed me.

No, I wasn't shocked, nor was I surprised. In fact, I'd expected it.

For several minutes, we stood together, arms around each other. She smelled faintly of lavender. I couldn't quite believe what was happening.

Finally she broke away, took my hand, and silently led me into the bedroom.

She pushed the door closed, walked over to the bed, turned to face me, and stood with her feet together, one knee slightly bent, like a model. She reached behind her and pulled something, and the dress slid to the floor. She was naked.

My throat went dry. I couldn't help it. I licked my lips, for God's sake, like a damn cat.

Everything, I mean *everything*, was exactly where it was supposed to be. She played tennis all right, and not just because of the instructors; she was fit. She had a six-pack that rivaled mine. She was tanned, and she was... waiting.

She was breathing quickly; her breasts were rising and falling.

"Oh please, come on. Forget the gloves, and the damn rules. I want *you*."

Gloves? Rules? What the hell is she talking about?

She took two steps toward me, stood up on tiptoe, and crushed her lips to mine. She grabbed my belt buckle, undid it, ripped the shirt out of my pants, and over my head. I didn't need any help with the pants, the boxers, or the shoes, and I am not one damned bit ashamed of what I did next. Put it down to research, if you like. I was on the job and this was a woman who didn't take no for an answer.

So I suffered in silence... well, not really in silence, and I sure as hell didn't suffer any, but you know what I mean. Then we lay there, on the bed, on our backs, staring up at the ceiling, and my brain was in overtime. I had questions, and I needed answers.

Gloves? Rules?

"What about your husband?"

"What about him?" She looked at me quizzically; her head tilted to one side so that she could see me.

"Isn't he likely to walk in on us?"

"Hah." She laughed. "No, of course not. This is my place. He never comes here, nor do I go to his."

"You live separately?"

"No, silly. We have a home on the mountain. He has one, too, you know."

"One what?"

"Pendant, of course." *Four! With her husband's, that's four of them.*

"Pendant?" I raised myself up onto my elbows, twisted toward her, and took her pendant in my fingers. "You mean this?"

'Yes, of course. What did you think I meant?"

"I don't know. I found mine. I was curious when I saw yours. What does it mean?"

"You *found* it? Oh my God." Her laughter echoed off the ceiling. "Darling, when you found that pendant it was your lucky day, not to mention mine. That pendant will open up a whole new and very exciting world for you."

She looked up at me, her eyes full of mischief, and said, "Come on, Harry. One more time, *pleeease.*"

"Why don't you tell me about the pendant?" I asked, changing the subject. "What does it mean?"

"Harry, when you hand your pendant to someone, like you handed yours to me at the club, or if someone simply shows their pendant to you, it's an invitation."

She looked at me through half-closed eyes.

"Go on."

"Okay. It all started with OM. Have you heard of OM, Harry? No? Well OM is all about Orgasmic Meditation. It's a business, perfectly legitimate, and they provide sex therapy, something for people who can't get off, mostly women. It's unique. Women, and men, so I'm told, buy into a fifteen-minute meditation session in which they take off their panties, or boxers, as the case may be. Then they lie down in a nest of pillows and have their... well, you know, stroked in very specific ways, usually by a man, but it could be a woman, wearing latex gloves. The stroker is called a research partner, a practitioner. But there are rules, no touching the research partner being the main one. Harry, I have to tell you, it was wonderful, at first. It did me a world of good, but then... well it is, after all, a business. The fifteen-minute sessions cost a fortune, and... Well, there was something missing. It doesn't go quite far enough. Then some bright soul, to whom I shall ever be grateful, came up with a new version. It's free. Yes, it has rules, but they're just guidelines pirated from OM. Touching... is optional. Are you with me so far?"

I nodded.

"So now we have Mystica, a version of kundalini, a club, if you will, which is represented by the pendant. Two serpents. Kundalini is a Sanskrit word that means coiled like a snake. Kundalini is said to be spiritual energy, the energy of the consciousness, that the gurus believe resides within the sleeping body. Access to it can only be achieved either through spiritual discipline or by spontaneously bringing about a new state of enhanced consciousness. They say that kundalini opens new pathways in the nervous system, that it's an awakening of a hidden treasure within. In our version, enhanced consciousness is achieved through, well... you know... Now do you understand?"

"I think so."

"Oh I *know* you do," she interrupted. "You sure as hell achieved advanced consciousness with me, and I know I did." She was laughing at me, and I couldn't help myself. I laughed, too.

"So you found it," she said, "the pendant. I was wondering why you weren't wearing it. It was a lie, wasn't it? The swimming thing?"

I nodded.

"The pendant is an open invitation to an invitation. Had you been wearing it, I could have invited you... and I would have. So... one more time, *please!*

I was done, and I said so. She pouted, and then grinned, flopping back on the pillows and closed her eyes.

"Olivia. Tell me about the members. How many are there? Who are they? Is Congressman Harper a member?"

"Oh no. We're not going there. You didn't get your pendant legitimately. I'm not giving away secrets to a private *dick*." At that, she giggled uncontrollably. "Besides," she gasped. "I think I want to keep you all to myself.

"Thank you, I think. But tell me, how did you get yours?"

"Oh, come on, Harry. Don't keep on... Okay, I was given

mine by a founding member. It's the only way you can get one. Membership is restricted and includes some very important people."

"Such as?"

She rolled over, looked at me, and said, "Not on your life, big boy."

We dressed, had a couple of drinks and, try as I might, I couldn't get another word about Mystica out of her, and try as *she* might, she couldn't get me back into bed, and she did try. Oh, how she tried.

It was after eight when I left her condo. I drove out of the gates, turned left onto Brainerd, and spotted the silver Honda SUV as it pulled away from the curb behind me. I slowed to give it a chance to catch up with me, but it turned away and disappeared at high speed.

Mystica? It's a damned sex club. I couldn't help but smile to myself. And then I thought of something else: Kate. *Damn it! I really screwed up this time... Research, that's what it was, research.*

22

The next morning, I called Kate. It wasn't a call I was looking forward to, but it had to be done. Over the phone? Whew, I didn't like to, but I didn't trust myself to tell her face-to-face about my encounter with the inimitable Olivia Hansen.

"Hey, Kate."

"Hi, Harry. What's up?"

"I have some news, about the pendant. My father found the woman at the club, the one he thought was wearing a copy of the pendant. She was. I did some research." I was glad she couldn't see me, then. *Research... sheesh.*

"I went to see her last night. Seems it's a key that gets you entry into some kind of weird, mystical society. Membership is invitation-only. I didn't get much out of her other than that, and that sex could be involved. The membership includes some very powerful people, but she wouldn't give me any names. Did you go to the gym?" *That's the way to do it; change the subject.*

"I did. It's just that, a gym. A very fancy one that seems

to cater only to Chattanooga's beautiful people; there were plenty of them there. I didn't join or work out. Didn't have time. But, sex? What does that mean?"

Damn!

"I think the club is a vehicle for discreet encounters between members. She told me that the pendant is a device they use to introduce themselves to each other. Weird, huh?"

"Very. Are we still on for tonight?"

"Dinner at Ducat? You bet. In fact, I'll give them a call and see if I need to make a reservation. Eight o'clock good for you?"

"Yes. Pick me up?"

"I'll be there at seven thirty."

She cut the connection, and I breathed a sigh of relief. I felt like shit.

23

I picked Kate up at seven thirty. She looked delicious in a simple, form-fitting gray dress, a matching knee-length overcoat and black shoes with three-inch heels.

Me? As always, I had kept it simple: white shirt, dark blue tie, navy blue blazer, and dark gray pants.

We arrived at La Maison Ducat right at eight. Only a few of the tables were occupied, but that wasn't surprising; it was Tuesday, after all.

Now I have to tell you, I've been in some fancy eateries in my time, and this one was right up there with the best of them.

It wasn't a big restaurant. There were perhaps fifteen or sixteen tables, all of them set for two, although they could all seat up to four people. The tables were covered with white linen, and the silverware was set for those who had been schooled by Emily Post: two knives and a spoon to the right, three forks to the left, a spoon and a fork at the head, a side plate with a butter knife, and three wine glasses. *Three,* for God's sake. *Thank the Lord for Mother Starke's tuition.*

There was a small bar just to the right, but no stools. Obviously, it was for use only by the wine waiters, one of whom arrived almost as soon as we sat down.

"The wine list, sir."

He handed it to me. It was a two-page list with perhaps twenty offerings; no prices. I smiled and ordered a bottle of Louis Latour Pinot Noir 2009.

"Good choice, sir. Excellent, in fact."

Kate grinned at me.

The wine arrived. I tasted it. He was right. It was good. I nodded. He poured, and then left us alone.

Five minutes later, the waiter arrived with the menu. It was table d'hôte, a choice of one of two set meals; again, no prices. We both settled for the rack of lamb with a *bouquetière* of mixed fresh vegetables. This was preceded by mock turtle soup, and the entre was followed by crème caramel dessert and, of course, coffee.

"What do you think?" I asked.

"The restaurant?" She looked around, frowned, and said, "Very nice, but you're right. It is a bit out of place for the area. I don't think there's anything quite like it anywhere else in the city."

"Well, you would know. So what the hell is a lowlife like Shady Tree doing owning a place like this?"

"I'd say he doesn't. He's probably fronting for someone else."

"He said he did, and the other businesses in the block, too." I shook my head, "But you're right. It doesn't work for me either."

"So if Tree doesn't own it, who does?"

"Harper would be my guess."

"What makes you think that?"

"It's a long story, and far from complete. Mike did the early spadework, but I have Ronnie on it now. Let's just say that there are a whole lot of shady dealings—no pun intended—going on in the Harper camp. Investments, fund transfers, banks, and all of it hidden under layers of shell and off-shore companies. There's no transparency or accountability at all. But there are indicators that Harper is in amongst it somewhere."

"Hey," she whispered, interrupting me, "don't be obvious; but try to get a look over to your right. Is that who I think it is?"

I dropped my napkin, bent down, picked it up, and looked across at the woman seated by herself two tables away. She was wearing glasses, and a dark blue, understated two-piece jacket and skirt, and shoes with modest heels.

"I dunno. Who do *you* think it is?"

"It's Senator Linda Michaels, chairman of the Senate Appropriations Committee. I've seen her on TV a bunch of times. There's even been talk that she might run for president."

"I dunno. Can't say I've ever seen her. I'm not into politics, you know that."

"Oh my God. Look at her neck."

This time, I turned in my seat. Sure enough, even from fifteen feet it was easy to make out the entwined snakes. I turned back to face Kate and nodded. She stared across the table at me, her eyes wide; an unspoken question. I thought for a moment.

"Okay, I'll get this. Give me a minute."

I got up from the table and went to the restroom. I took off my tie and put it in my pocket, and then I put the pendant around my neck and made sure the collar of my shirt was open far enough for it to be easily seen. I checked how I looked in the mirror, and then headed back into the dining area.

As I passed her table, I made it a point to look down at the senator, and then I did a rather obvious double take, turned, and approached her table.

"Senator Michaels?"

She looked up. "Yes?"

I leaned forward and offered her my hand, letting the pendant swing out from inside my shirt. "It's so good to see you in person, ma'am. I'm a big admirer."

She continued to look up at me; no, she was looking at the pendant. She smiled, took my hand, quite firmly, and shook it, once.

"It's nice to see you, too, Mr..."

"Starke, ma'am. Harry Starke."

I was able to get a better look at her; the suit was, I thought, a little deceiving. I had a feeling there was more to Senator Michaels than met the eye.

"Nice to meet you, Mr. Starke. Thank you for your attention and support."

"No, ma'am, thank *you* for all that you do." I looked over at Kate, who was watching closely.

"What do you do, Mr. Starke?" Her voice had a pleasant resonance to it. "Should I know you?"

"I wouldn't think so, Senator. I work for my father." *Not exactly a lie, but what the hell.*

"Your father? And what does he do?"

"He's lawyer, ma'am, a tort lawyer, and a very good one."

The senator nodded. "Do you have a card, Mr. Starke?"

"I do." I gave her one of what I call my anonymous cards: it had my name and cell phone number on it, but no profession or company affiliation. She took it, looked at it, nodded, slipped the card into her clutch, and offered me her hand. I took it, and immediately felt a slight pressure from her forefinger on the center of my palm.

"Thank you, Mr. Starke. It was very nice to meet you. I do hope you have a lovely evening."

"Thank *you*, Senator."

"You dog, Harry," Kate said as I sat down. "What was that all about?"

"Just testing the waters. Her pendant is a twin to this one. She got a good look at it. We'll see what happens, if anything."

"Yeah," she said, "and there's more. Look at that picture over there."

There was a lot of art on the walls. "Where? Which one?"

"The door, over there in the rear wall, over the top of it. There's a small painting. Look at it."

I did, and I saw what she was talking about; a small painting, maybe fifteen inches square. It wasn't a picture of anything in particular, just patterns. That's what I thought at first. The colors were muted pastels, mostly shades of blue and pink. I had to look hard to make anything of it. The distance made it difficult to make out the patterns, but it was there, right in the middle, barely discernable amid the rest of the swirls, two snakes entwined, each swallowing the other's tail. I turned and looked at Kate. She was grinning.

"Geez, Kate. It can't be a coincidence. There's something weird going on."

She nodded. "You know, Harry, now that I think about it, I'm almost certain there's one just like it over a door in the rear wall of the gym. I saw it yesterday, but didn't take any notice then. The patterns are difficult to see. You have to know what you're looking for, and I didn't, at least not then. We need to check out the other businesses."

"It's a bit late now. It's after ten. They're all closed, except for this one and the gym. Besides, I can't. Shady and his boys know me too well."

She nodded. "They don't know me. I'll see if I can join the gym. I'll do it tomorrow."

Our meal lasted for another thirty minutes, during which time Senator Michaels finished her meal and left. She nodded to us as she walked out of the front door. She was a good-looking woman.

I called for the check. *Wow! $392; talk about sticker shock. This is no place for a quiet night out. Only a millionaire can afford these prices.* I paid the bill, left a tip that was more than I would normally pay for the meal, and left with Kate just after ten thirty. The door under the painting at the rear of the dining room remained closed the whole time we were there. No one went in; no one came out.

I took Kate home, kissed her goodnight, watched as she walked to her door and let herself in. Then I drove home. The city was quiet, the streets almost deserted. My head was in a whirl. I was half-expecting a call from the senator, but no. I poured myself three fingers of liquid gold, wandered into the living room, and sat for ten minutes and looked out over the river, thinking about the events of the day, and then I went to bed. Sleep did not come easily, and when it did, my dreams were full of snakes, dark water, and... Senator Linda Michaels.

24

The following morning, I got to the office late. Jacque immediately loaded me with paperwork. I got most of it done and out of the way and was enjoying a second cup of coffee when my office door opened.

"Lieutenant Gazzara is here to see you, Mr. Starke," Jacque said, standing to one side to let her in.

"Hey, Kate. What's up?"

"This is official, Harry. I need you to come with me."

I rose to my feet. "What the hell? Why?"

"She's dead, Harry. Olivia Hansen is dead."

I was dumbstruck. My mind went blank. Time seemed to stand still. I couldn't think. *Dead? What the hell happened?* Then I came out of it.

"Oh shit. Where? When? How?"

"Later, Harry. Let's go."

We left everyone in the office staring after us. Lonnie Guest was waiting outside, standing beside the unmarked, waiting, a huge grin on his face.

"Told ya, didn't I, Starke?" he said, opening the rear door. "I told you we'd get ya. Welcome to the dark side."

"Shut up, Sergeant." Kate glared at him. I got in the car and Lonnie slammed the door shut, still with that shit-eating grin on his face.

The receptionist at the police department on Amnicola buzzed us in, and I was taken straight back to an interview room. Kate and I sat down, one on either side of the table. Lonnie lounged against the wall with his legs crossed at the ankles and his arms folded across his chest. He was one happy detective.

Kate turned on the recorder and the camera, went through the usual routine, identified those present, recorded the date and time and so on, and then it began.

"Where were you on the afternoon and evening of Monday, January twenty-sixth?"

"You know where I was. I told you. I was with Olivia Hansen, at her condo in Alderney Gardens."

"What time did you arrive at Alderney Gardens?"

"Just after five."

"Why were you there?"

"I told you. I wanted to find out about the pendant, Tabitha Willard's pendant."

"How did that go? Did you learn anything?"

"I did. But not enough. It's a key, admission to some kind of sex club."

Lonnie sniggered. Kate looked sharply at him.

"And?"

"That was about it. She wouldn't tell me anything about it. How did she die? When?"

"She was strangled. The ME puts the time of death

sometime between seven and midnight. That gives you opportunity, Harry."

"Of course it does, but I didn't do it."

"He thinks you did." She nodded her head in Lonnie's direction.

"He's a stupid f... He's stupid."

"Yup, that's why I'm here and you're there." Lonnie grinned as he said it. I'd never seen the man so happy.

"You were there a long time, Harry. Why?"

"Hell, Kate. She didn't want to talk about it. I had to be persuasive. It took time."

"You were there from five until eight," she said. "That's three hours. It took three hours? Did you have intimate relations with her?"

"That's none of your business."

"It is my business. This is a murder investigation, and you're a person of interest. Now don't lie to me. Did you have intimate relations with Olivia Hansen?"

"No comment."

"Fine. Then you should know that the ME determined that she engaged in sexual intercourse no more than ten hours before her death. I think you had sex with her and as far as we know, you were the last one to see her alive. Your prints are all over her condo; only yours, Harry."

They didn't know that I had sex with her; not for sure, but they soon would. A DNA test would confirm it, so I didn't need to qualify or deny it.

"Of course my prints were there; I was there. And so was someone else. There must have been, because I didn't kill her."

"And who might that have been?"

"Hell, I don't know. I left around eight, and I was followed, well, for a short distance, by a silver Honda SUV."

"Hah!" Lonnie said. "Don't that beat all? You were followed. Of course you were, dumb ass." Hell, he wasn't even good at sarcasm.

"Kate, you know I didn't kill that woman. So what's this about?"

"Just crossing the *t*'s and dotting the *i*'s, Harry. You know the routine."

"The hell you say," Lonnie growled. "He did it. Sure as hell, he did."

Kate shook her head. "Maybe, but probably not. You can go, Harry."

She followed me out into the parking lot. Amnicola Highway was busy. It was just after eleven o'clock.

"Buy you a coffee?" I asked.

She looked at me, nodded. "Over there."

We walked across the busy road to McDonalds, ordered coffee, and sat down at a table by the window.

"Come on, Kate. Give."

"You say she had a pendant. Was she wearing it? Did you take it?"

"Yes, she was, and no, I didn't take it."

"Well, it was gone, Harry." She sat quietly for a moment, sipping her coffee. "I don't think for one minute you killed her, but you're in way over your head this time. You screwed her, Harry, possibly only minutes before she died. That makes you a suspect."

I looked down at my coffee and said nothing.

"Do you have any idea who could have killed her?"

I shook my head, slowly, and then looked her in the eye.

"So, if we know that you didn't do it, and that you left

around eight, that narrows the time of death to the four hours before midnight. Someone got past the gate, but not in a car. The guard doesn't remember any other car, known or unknown to him, entering or leaving the complex, other than yours. The security cameras confirm that, too."

"It's only a gated community, Kate, not Fort Knox. Someone could have walked in."

"Not through the gate. The cameras would have recorded any intruders."

"Then they must have gone over the wall."

"That's what I think. And somewhere between there and her front door, whoever it was stepped in something nasty. By the time he or she arrived at the door, the shoe was almost clean; it left just a faint, partial print in the foyer floor. A Nike tennis shoe. They figure the size to be between nine and eleven. You wear Nikes and you're size eleven, Harry."

I nodded. "Along with half the men in the state. Go on."

"She must have known whoever it was, because there's no sign of forced entry."

"Not necessarily. It's supposed to be a secure community. That being so, it's possible she opened the door and whoever it was shoved it open. Hell, maybe she had a date. The pendant."

Kate nodded. "That's possible. The maid found her on the bed. She was naked, strangled. Unfortunately, whoever killed her knew what he was doing. No traces or anything. He must have worn gloves, coveralls, maybe even a hairnet. According to what little evidence we have, you were her only visitor that night."

"So where do we go from here?"

"With the investigation, you mean? We keep digging. You need to stay on track with Harper. Keep me informed.

I'll do what I do and if I have anything I can share, I will. As far as you and me..."

Oh oh, here it comes.

She was silent for a long moment. I waited.

"I don't know. I just don't know. Harry, I've never had any illusions about you. You've always been one to cat around, and I've always looked the other way—well, most of the time. But *this*..."

"You're right, Kate. I am what I am, and yes, I have gone off the rails a time or two, but you're the only one in my life who matters. What I said the other day about research, it was true, at least at first. I figured it was like water boarding, a necessary evil to get the information I needed, and then... well, it kinda got out of hand."

"It got out of hand all right. Water boarding? Sheesh. That's a good one. Water boarding! I'll have to remember that." She shook her head, slowly and sadly.

"Kate, I'm forty-two years old..."

"Dammit, I *know* that, Harry." She looked around; people were listening. She lowered her voice. "We've never made each other any promises, which was fine, but... Harry, I think we've reached a sad place in our relationship. I think we need to take a break."

"Kate..."

"No. Hear me out. I think we need to take a break. I know I do. I need to think. In the meantime, as a professional, I'll continue to work with you, help you when I can, and I expect you to do the same. We're a good team, Harry. We work well together, but on a personal level—well, I can't do this anymore. I need some time. Like I said, I'll keep working with you. Outside of that, it's 'don't call me, I'll call you.'"

With that she pushed her cup to one side and headed out of the restaurant. I watched through the window as she ran across Amnicola and into the police department.

What the hell have I done?

I sipped on what was left in my cup. I can't tell you quite how I felt, but it wasn't good: kind of wrung out, guilty, stupid, whatever.

It wasn't the first time something like this had happened, but never before had I been caught quite so... red-handed. Not only that, I was in something of a mess. I was in the middle of an investigation that included a suicide and two murders and Kate was *the* major player. On top of all that, I had the Harper thing to deal with. Dammit.

Yeah, I was upset that she'd walked on me, but she's done it before. She'd be back, I hoped. *But then again, she's never caught me screwing someone else before. Well, she has... but this time it's different. Geez. Oh well—what's done is done. I can't change it, so I'll just have to let it play out and hope for the best.*

There was nothing I could do about the two murders. My office didn't have the resources to carry out a full-fledged murder investigation, and it wasn't my job anyway. Kate and dumbass would have to handle that. All I could do was work on my investigation for Willard and continue to dig into Harper and his foundation, but here's the quandary: I was pretty damn sure that the suicide, murders, and the foundation were all somehow connected. If so, a large part of what I needed to do was beyond my sphere of operations... or was it?

I dragged out my iPhone and flipped the lock screen. *Damn, it's still only Wednesday.*

25

For the next couple of days I occupied myself with the routine matters of the agency. Harper wasn't the only thing I had on my mind, and I'd been neglecting my duties, which vexed Jacque no end.

I spent the days catching up and mulling over what I thought I knew, though it wasn't much. I thought a lot about what had happened to Olivia. Someone was going to pay for that. I didn't hear a word from Kate.

On Friday morning I called the staff into the conference room. We did the usual rundown of the week's progress, and then the conversation turned to Harper. Ronnie and Tim both allowed that they were making progress, but neither one was ready to report. I was frustrated, but it was no good pushing them. They did what they did, and they always got it right, which was why I'd hired them. I closed the meeting, got myself a cup of coffee, and went back to roost in my office.

Dammit! I have to do *something. Can't just sit here and mope.... Olivia.... Who killed her? Why? And Charlie.* I shuddered at the thought. *What the hell would have happened if I hadn't pushed her away? Wow.* Now there was something to ponder.

Falk! Who killed Falk? Why? What did he do? What did he... The gun was a 9 mm. Gold has a 9 mm!

I sat up straight. It was time for another visit to Shady. I needed to get my hands on that gun. Kate needed to get her hands on it. It could provide an answer to who killed Falk. If it *was* a match for the one that killed Falk, we'd have him, and Tree, and maybe Harper, too, if Tree talked. If it wasn't a match... well, no harm done. It would take a bit of figuring out, but either way it was a win-win.

I didn't say anything to anyone in the office. What I was about to do could get me into some deep trouble, and not just with the law; I could get hurt, or worse.

It was about four o'clock that afternoon when I arrived at the mall. The restaurant was closed, the gym was busy, and so was the cigar store. The two clothing outlets, not so much.

I circled the block, through the parking lot on McCallie, from south to north, then swung around the block and did the same at the rear. And there it was. Outside what I knew must be the rear entrance to Shady's office sat the Beemer that had followed me on Saturday evening, after I'd left my father at the club.

I hit the Bluetooth and called Kate. God only knew what kind of reception I would get. Maybe she wouldn't even take the call.

"What do you want, Harry? I'm busy." Wow. Her voice was like ice.

"Yeah, well. I think I have something that might interest you. I'm at the mall on McCallie. The other day, when I came by to get compensation from Shady for the injury to Mike's nose—"

"Robbed him at gunpoint, you mean."

"No, Kate. I never touched my gun." It was a lie, but what the hell, I was in over my head in trouble with her anyway. One more little untruth wasn't going to make it any worse.

"No? Then you must have beat it out of him with that baton of yours."

"Whatever. I never touched him. Just listen to me for a minute, will you? While I was there, I did have occasion to subdue his cronies, Stimpy and Ren."

She almost giggled, but not quite. "So?"

"Gold was wearing a rig with a 9 mm."

Silence, then, "Did you get it?"

"Err... no. I guess he still has it."

"Pity. I can't touch it. Not without probable cause."

"You can't, but I can."

"Harry, I don't like where this is going."

"Look, Kate. If he threatens me with it, I can take it away from him, and then I can hand it over to you. I would be doing my civic duty, right?"

"I don't like it, Harry. I'd rather do it with a warrant, and I can't get one without cause."

"Okay. How about this? Judge Strange owes me a favor. Suppose I get you cause? He would issue a warrant, right? Tell you what. You come on down to the mall and meet me outside."

"What, right now?"

"You want the gun or not?"

"Okay, I'm at Amnicola. Give me twenty."

"Great. If I'm not waiting for you outside, come on in and rescue me. I'll leave the door open for you."

She disconnected. I grinned. *Just like old times. Twenty, huh? This has to be timed just right.*

I parked the car outside the front of Shady's office and dumped the nine in the glove box. There was a newspaper on the back seat of the car. I folded it twice, looked at my watch, and waited exactly thirteen minutes. I figured I'd have just enough time to do what needed to be done before Kate arrived. Then I got out of the car, locked it, and headed for the front door with the newspaper held behind my back. I pushed the bell button.

The door was opened by my fat friend from my previous visits. He took one look at me and turned and ran down the passageway to Shady's office.

Predictable.

I bent down and put the newspaper against the bottom of the door jamb and allowed the door to close on it. It did, but not quite. There was a quarter-inch gap, just enough to get a finger inside and pull it open.

To say they were surprised to see me was an understatement. This fat man already had his back to the wall, just inside the door. Duvon and Gold both pulled their weapons. Tree ripped open his desk drawer and grabbed one of his own.

"Whoa! Dammit, Shady. What kind of hello is that?" I had my hands held high, palms facing them, my coat open to reveal the empty rig.

"You son of a bitch. I told you never to come back here. I oughta cap your ass. What the hell do you want this time? You bring my money back?"

"I just have a couple of questions. We have three dead

bodies, two of them homicides. I know you don't go for murder, Shady, but Harper... I need to know about you and Congressman Harper. What's the connection, Shady?

I thought he was going to burst. He could barely speak he was so angry.

"You—you—you piece o' crap. I don't have to tell you nothin'."

"Now, Shady..."

"Shut the *hell* up, you piece o' *shit*. You think you can waltz in here any time you want? Screw you, you... you... Duvon, go smack him upside the head, hard."

Duvon took a step forward. "I'll kill his ass."

"I said smack him, not kill him, you stupid, dumbass son of a bitch."

Duvon looked at him like he'd been smacked himself. I wasn't surprised. I'm not quite as stupid as it might appear. I knew Shady was no killer, but his two idiot cronies? Maybe. Be that as it may, Duvon duly smacked me. At least he tried to. I knew it was coming and I held up my right arm. It took the blow, and it hurt like hell. I thought for a moment that he might have broken my wrist. He raised the gun for another try.

"That's enough. Drop 'em. All of you."

Kate walked in, her gun pointed right at Shady's face. She was followed by Lonnie, who still had that same goofy smile on his face.

"Get out of here, Harry," Kate said, without taking her eyes off the three amigos.

"But—"

"No buts. Out. Now."

I didn't argue. I left. I waited outside, sitting on the hood of the Maxima.

They came out about five minutes later, empty-handed.

"Well?"

"No good, Harry. Gold's gun was a small-frame Ruger. Tree's was a 9 mm, a Smith and Wesson. Falk was killed with a Beretta. Duvon's gun? A damned great .45, a cannon. All of their weapons are perfectly legal. The permits are all in order. Waste of time, Harry."

I rubbed my arm. It was going to be sore for a while. "Dammit."

She smiled and shook her head. "Better luck next time, Harry."

Then she and Lonnie got into their car and drove away. No goodbye, nothing.

I guess I'm still in the doghouse. What the hell do I do now?

26

I got into the office early the following morning, Saturday, before eight. I did some routine chores, paperwork, made a couple of calls feeling kind of like a fish out of water the whole time. I wasn't used to not having Kate around. I made myself a cup of coffee and then just sat there, alone with the Dark Italian roast and my thoughts. My cell phone rang. It was ten o'clock.

"Harry Starke."

"Ah, Mr. Starke. You're there."

I sat bolt upright in my chair. She had my full attention.

"Senator Michaels?"

"Yes. Do you have a minute?"

"I do. How can I help you?"

"I think it's more what I can do for you, or at least for Mr. Starke Senior."

"Er... what do you mean?"

"I think I might have something for him, but I wanted to run it by you first. Could you meet me, this evening, perhaps?"

"Well, yes... of course, but wouldn't it be better if you spoke directly to my father?"

"It might, but I'd rather talk to you first, if you don't mind, just to make sure that what I have in mind wouldn't be a waste of his time. I'm sure you would know."

"All right. What did you have in mind?"

"Why dinner, of course, at that nice little restaurant where we met the other day, my treat. Would that suit you?"

I almost laughed out loud. "Yes, ma'am, that would suit me fine. What time would you like me to pick you up, and where?"

"I took the liberty of making a reservation for ten o'clock. Is that too late?"

"Not at all. I'll pick you up... where?"

"I'm staying at the Read House. Shall we say nine o'clock? That will give us time for a drink before the meal."

"Nine o'clock it is."

"Good. I'll be in the lobby. Goodbye, Mr. Starke." She cut the connection, and I sat back in my chair and smiled.

Something for my father, my ass!

I was ready to go an hour early. I couldn't stay still, not for a minute. I'd been that way all day. I couldn't concentrate on anything but my impending date—if it was a date. I paced, watched TV, and fidgeted. I was excited, and not a little apprehensive. After all, it's not every day that one gets to dine with a United States senator, now is it?

It's very rare that I bother to dress up, and by that I mean in a suit and tie. Don't get the wrong idea. I dress well most of the time, but I prefer more casual clothes. The grungy gear I wear mostly at night, when I'm trolling the nightclubs and bars. That way I blend in. On rare occasions, though, I do make the effort; and this, I figured, was one of those occasions.

I chose a navy blue two-piece suit with a white, V-neck cashmere sweater—the idea being to show off my pendant. I felt like a damned turkey, cooked and dressed for the table. *Oh well. Sometimes we all have to make sacrifices.* I smiled at the thought. *Some sacrifice.*

It was exactly nine o'clock when I parked the car out front of the Read House and went inside.

Now, before I go any further, you should know that I'd done a little research on our good lady senator. She was fifty-two, hails from Boston, and is tipped to one day make a run for the presidency. Yes, she's that important, and when I walked through that door and saw her, I had no doubt she could win it. I have to admit, I was more than a little intimidated.

She was waiting for me in the lobby. She couldn't have been there long, because she was standing by the reception desk. She was taller than I'd thought, and she was wearing four-inch heels that lifted her close to six feet two. She didn't look a day over forty. The glasses were gone. The skin was smooth. Her figure was well proportioned and, so I assumed by the fit of her clothes, it needed no help from foundation garments. Her dark brown hair framed her face, covered her ears, and was cut so that it just brushed her shoulders. She wasn't the most beautiful woman in the room, but she was the most attractive, and she owned it.

She was wearing a pale blue, waist-length satin jacket that shimmered under the lights over a black cocktail dress cut two inches above the knee. She carried a pale blue leather clutch, an exact match for the jacket.

She walked confidently across the lobby to meet me, took my arm and together we walked out into the night. She'd not yet said a word, not even hello. I was more than a little conscious of the looks we received as we left the hotel.

I opened the car door for her, and she slid into the front seat. I closed the door and went around to the driver's side, got in, and pushed the starter.

"Good evening, Mr. Starke. You look... different."

I looked at her and smiled. "Please, call me Harry. Different?"

"Yes. You look very nice. Shall we go?"

We did.

It was a Saturday night, so Ducat was quite busy, but she didn't seem perturbed. We were escorted to a table that had obviously been chosen for its seclusion. It was at the front, at the extreme right corner of the restaurant; she sat with her back to the room. The only view anyone would have of her was her hair and shoulders; the chairs had high backs. The good senator had obviously done this before. The maître d' took her coat. I slipped him a twenty; he smiled, dipped his head, and left us alone.

Okay, I said she wasn't the most beautiful woman in the Read House lobby, but in that restaurant? Oh yeah. The cocktail dress she wore was strapless, and she filled it beautifully. We were seated opposite one another, and I couldn't help myself; I couldn't take my eyes off her.

"Harry," she whispered with a smile. "It's rude to stare."

"Yes, ma'am. It certainly is, and I'm sorry... No, no I'm

not," again the smile, "but you look a little different yourself. That's quite a dress, and, if I may be so bold, Senator, that's quite a woman inside it."

She laughed, quietly. "Well said, Harry, and thank you. It's a rare thing to encounter a man with balls enough to say what's on his mind, much less hand me a compliment—one that doesn't have strings attached, that is. Please, Harry. My name is Linda. No more ma'am or senator, agreed?"

Balls? Methinks that maybe the senator is no lady. If she is, she's a damned tough one.

I smiled back at her. "Yes, ma'am."

That brought another low laugh.

"Would you like to see the wine list, sir?"

I looked up at the wine waiter and opened my mouth to speak, but before I could, she said, "No thank you, Louis. I'll have a vodka tonic, my friend will have a gin and tonic, Bombay Sapphire with a small square of lime, and we'll have a bottle of Opus One with the meal."

Louis nodded and backed away. I looked at her. The question on my face must have been obvious.

"Oh come on, Harry. You don't think for one minute that I wouldn't have you checked out, did you? I know exactly who you are, and what you do. In fact, I probably know more about you than you do. I even know what brand of toothpaste you use. Work for your father, my ass. You're a private investigator, and a very good one, so I'm told. I might add that I need your word that everything said between us tonight stays between us."

"Of course."

"Good. Then let's enjoy our meal and our time together. I need a damned break from the rabble I find myself constantly surrounded by, and I'm sure you do, too... and that brings me to the next item. How is that lovely young thing I saw you with the other day? A detective, isn't she? Are you two an item?"

I shrugged my shoulders. I couldn't believe this woman. "She is, and we were, but not anymore. She's fine, I think."

"Well, now you're single. Isn't that a turn up for the books?"

She leaned back in her chair, sipped her drink, and smiled at me over the rim of the glass. I felt so out of my damned depth, so uncomfortable... and why wouldn't? I was sitting in a restaurant, alone with one of the most powerful women in the world.

"Harry, you look very uptight. You must learn to relax. You'll spoil our evening together. We'll have a nice meal; the chef here is amazing. Let's unwind and enjoy ourselves. Agreed?"

"Agreed, but I thought you wanted to talk business."

"I do, but later. For now... Ah, here's François."

Yep, she knows this place, well.

"Good evening, Madam." He slid her napkin out of the silver band for her, shook it open, draped it over her lap, then took the menu from under his arm and handed it to her. She passed it over to me without looking at it. It was another set menu with two choices.

"I'm going to have the *sole bonne femme*, Harry. They serve it over wild rice. The sauce is delicious. You should try it."

Well, if it's good enough for her....

"Sounds good. I'll have that, too, please, François."

"Thank you, sir. Louis will bring your wine shortly. Would you like another cocktail before it arrives?"

I looked at her. She shook her head.

"No, thank you. We'll wait for the wine."

All that time I had a strange feeling that I was performing a part in some sort of weird ritual. Kate and I had not been treated the way Linda and I were being treated. But then, the lady was a United States senator.

Maybe that's the reason for the VIP treatment. She doesn't seem to mind being seen with me in public. Then there's that damned pendant, and where are the Secret Service? Surely they don't let her loose on her own.

"Linda." I was having a tough time with that, too, using her first name. "I have to ask, where are the Secret Service? I can't believe they'd let you out of their sight."

She smiled. "They don't. Look there." She pointed through the slats of the blinds that covered the window, and there it was: a discreet, black, four-door Cadillac. Now I really was intimidated, and it must have showed, because I was treated to another of her low laughs.

"Oh, stop it, Harry. Of course I have protection, but there's nothing to worry about. The three agents out there have been with me for a long time. I love them all. They know me very well, and they are *very* discreet."

What the hell am I getting myself into?

"Ah, here's the pate. Do you like foie gras?"

Thank God I know what the hell she's talking about.

The waiter placed a small plate in front of each of us. On it was a small, perfectly round portion of foie gras; it looked as if it had been turned out of a mold, and it probably had. Each portion was accompanied by four fingers of warm, unbuttered toast folded in a white napkin.

"Actually I do, but we don't see it very often here in the South. Southern folk don't like goose liver, or any other kind of liver. This looks wonderful." And it was, and so was the sole; the fish was cooked to perfection, followed by a white chocolate crème brûlée for dessert.

It was almost eleven thirty when we finished the meal, but the night was not yet over. The restaurant was almost empty. Just one other couple remained; they were enjoying a final cup of coffee three tables away.

"Coffee, Harry?"

"No, I don't think so, thank you."

"How about some brandy then?"

I thought about it, and then nodded.

She attracted Louis's attention and ordered Domaine Dupont Calvados, whatever that was. I'd never heard of it, but it was smooth, and a perfect end to a perfect evening.

"I'll get the check." I reached for my wallet.

She chuckled. "It's already paid for, Harry, and so is the tip. I have an account here. I did say it was my treat."

"Yes, you did, but—"

"Harry. Enough!"

I sighed and shook my head. "Okay." I looked around. "I suppose we should leave."

"What on earth for?"

I squinted, frowned, and looked her in the eye. I didn't have to ask. My question was obvious.

"You'll see. Be patient."

We waited until the restaurant was empty. The last couple left at a little after midnight. She rose from her seat, and François rushed over with her jacket. She didn't bother to put it on.

"Come with me."

"What about...?" I nodded in the direction of the black car outside.

"Oh, don't worry about them. They'll leave when I do."

I raised my eyebrows, but she didn't elaborate.

I got up from my seat and followed her to the door in the rear wall, the one with the painting of the two serpents over it. There was an audible click. Someone, somewhere, had pushed a button. We walked through into a passageway that ran the entire length of the rear of the building. She turned left. At the end of the passageway was a flight of stairs that led to the upper floor and another passageway that ran the length of the front of the building. It reminded me of a hotel. There were doors at intervals from one end to the other.

She walked ahead of me, her hips rolling gently under her tight black dress. I could see the outline of every muscle. *High heels really do something for a woman, don't they?*

The doors weren't numbered, but she seemed to know which one she wanted. She stopped, withdrew a key card from her clutch and she swiped it through the lock. The door opened, and she stepped inside. I followed.

Now I knew what the mall was all about. Apart from providing Shady with an office, a place from which to conduct his business, it was also a place for like-minded people to get together. The fact that the five outlets on the ground floor made money was an added bonus.

We were inside a small luxury suite, with a large bedroom, a sitting room, a bathroom, utilities for making coffee, and a small but well-stocked bar.

"Make yourself at home, Harry. Pour the drinks. Sorry, I don't have any Laphroaig." She smiled as she said it.

I grinned and shook my head. "What can I get for you?"

"Vodka tonic; easy on the ice."

She tossed her jacket onto a chair by the door.

"I'll be just a minute." She stepped into the bathroom.

I poured the drinks and sat down to wait.

After a moment, I heard the toilet flush, and then the sound of running water.

"Now then, Harry." She took the drink from my hand and sat down on a chair directly opposite me. She looked me squarely in the eye and said, "We're alone now so we can talk freely."

"You sure?"

"What do you mean? Oh, you mean... Don't worry. This place is swept for bugs on a regular basis. It's secure."

Again, I wondered what I'd gotten myself into, but what the hell. Here I was, alone with a beautiful woman. Why not enjoy the moment?

"You said you might have something for my father."

"And you believed me, didn't you? *Really,* Harry." The sarcasm was unmistakable. "What the hell did you think I would do when you dangled that thing in front of my face? Offer you a job? Be serious. You knew exactly what you were doing, but you weren't expecting anything, were you? After all, very few men on this planet get to screw a sitting United States senator, especially this one. And you're not there yet."

I was speechless, struck dumb.

"Oh, don't look so shocked. You know the ropes."

I do?

"You know what this place is. As I said, it's secure. I come here every once in a while, mostly just to rest, to get away from it all. I'm not married; well, I'm a widow, as you probably know. I don't engage in casual relationships. I can't afford to. Mystica was a gift from the Gods, an answer to many of my needs, needs that are unique to me and what I am, and before you ask the obvious question: only once before have I brought a man to this apartment. This is my refuge, a place to be alone, and to think. Although, it does provide a unique opportunity, should I ever need to... Well. I'll let you figure it out."

She sipped her drink, staring at me over the rim of the glass. She put the drink down on the coffee table, leaned forward, put her elbows on her knees and clasped her hands together in front of her.

"I'm going to ask you a question, and I want you to think very carefully before you answer it. Don't lie to me. If you do... Tell me, why are you a member of Mystica?"

I didn't even have to think about it. "I'm not."

"Not what? Not going to tell me?"

"I'm not a member, Linda. Never have been, never will be."

"But you have the pendant."

"I do, but... well..."

"Tell me, Harry. What you say next—"

I interrupted her, "Linda, it doesn't even belong to me. It belongs to a young woman who committed suicide. I've been retained by her father to investigate what happened to her. She was wearing it around her neck when they took her out of the water. When I spotted your pendant the other night, I had to try and find out what it meant. Look, if you want me to go, I will." I started to rise, but she waved her hand for me to sit down again.

I'm not sure, but I thought I saw her breathe a sigh of relief.

"I believe you, Harry." She picked up her drink, took a sip, and then set it down again.

"Now." I looked at her. "Can I ask you the same question?"

She shook her head. "No."

"Why not?"

"For several reasons, the foremost of which is that I don't want you to. Another is because I don't want to become part of your investigation."

"I understand. I do need to know about Mystica, though."

"Then you'll have to find out from someone else. That should be easy enough for a man of your talents."

I didn't press the point. I was happy just to still be there.

She downed the rest of her drink, got up from the chair, and walked over to the bar.

"Would you like another, Harry?"

"Better not. I'm driving."

"No you're not. You've already had too much to be allowed to drive home, much less drive me back to the hotel, and my friends have already left for the night. Same again?"

I looked at my watch. It was already past twelve thirty. "Sure, why not?"

We talked for maybe another thirty minutes, though I wasn't watching the time. Mostly, I was watching her, and she was asking questions; she was relentless.

"Are you in love with your detective friend, Harry?"

It was on the tip of my tongue to give her a quick answer, but something made me pause. I lowered my head so she couldn't see my eyes, and I thought about it. Was I? I'd always thought so, but then I realized something, and I looked up at her. She was watching me intently. I took a deep breath. *Here we go.*

"Linda, I have known Kate for a long time, more than fifteen years. We've been seeing each other for almost ten years and, until you asked me that question, I really thought I was in love with her, but then I realized something. Ten years and I'd never asked her to marry me, and she's never mentioned it either. No, I'm not in love with Kate."

She nodded. "Good. I believe you. I need to use the restroom. I'll be just a moment."

I sat back in the chair and gazed up at the ceiling. Again, the toilet flushed, the water ran, and then I looked down and there she was.

Oh. My. God.

She was standing in the backlight from the bathroom. The dress was gone. She was posed like some super model. All she had on was a black strapless bra and tiny black panties so sheer I could see right through them, and she was still wearing her heels.

Now I have to tell you, I'd been fantasizing about where I hoped the night might be going, but that's all it was: a fantasy. Never in my wildest imaginings did I expect anything to actually happen. She glided across the room, kicked off the shoes, and then she sat down on my lap. I could barely breathe, and it wasn't because she was heavy; she wasn't.

I put my arm around her waist. Her skin was cold, but it felt like silk. She put her hands together on my shoulder and leaned her head on them, breathing gently, as if she was about to go to sleep. I could smell her perfume, and I know it sounds stupid, but I actually wondered if that was what heaven must smell like.

We sat like that for a long time, saying nothing. I thought for a moment she'd fallen asleep, but then she sat up and looked into my eyes.

"Make love to me, Harry."

It was after nine the following morning we I drove her back to the Read House. The black Caddy followed at a discreet distance. I pulled up outside the front entrance to the hotel. She leaned over and gave me a peck on the cheek.

"Thank you, Harry. I had a lovely time. I hope you did, too. Until the next time, then?"

She didn't give me a chance to answer. She flung open the car door, swung herself out, and then breezed in through the front door. I could only sit there and shake my head.

What the hell has just happened to me? Better yet: there's going to be a next time. Oh my God. Thank you, Lord.

I put the car in drive and pulled away from the front of the hotel. My intention was to continue on MLK to the interchange on Highway 27, but as I cruised past the multi-level parking lot, I also drove past the silver Honda. I didn't notice it until I was alongside it. Maybe I was tired, distracted by thoughts of my oh-so-amazing experience. I don't know. Whatever it was, my reactions were slow. I must have driven twenty yards past the Honda when I caught on. I slammed on the brakes, jammed the car into reverse, and floored the gas pedal. I almost hit the Honda as it made a right on Walnut and screamed away. By the time I made the turn and went after it, it was gone. Disappeared.

What the hell?

I cruised around several adjacent blocks, but there was no sign of it.

Damn!

27

It had been a rough week—well, with the exception of my dinner with Linda Michaels. I hadn't heard from Kate since Wednesday. I'd done my best to put our differences out of my mind—*differences? That's a joke*—and concentrate on what had happened to Tabitha, Falk, and now Olivia. There wasn't much to go on. The only straw I had was what Ronnie and Mike were doing, and they still had nothing to share with me. I also had the senator on my mind. I'd half a thought that I might hear from her, but I hadn't.

Just after ten on Sunday morning, I was on my third cup of coffee, relaxing on the sofa. I looked out over the river. It was one of those bleak, cold and utterly miserable days. The sky was concealed by a low-lying blanket of cloud that was, itself, all but hidden by a driving, horizontal rain that was coming down in torrents, whipping the surface of the river to foam and battering the windows. It was a good day to stay home and do nothing, so that's what I did. I lay stretched out on the sofa for most of the morning, drinking coffee, reading the newspaper, watching the rain, thinking... about Linda, Kate, and Harper. Always Harper.

It was almost noon when my cell phone rang. I looked at the screen. It was Kate. I smiled. I don't know why, but I did. If nothing else, I wanted her as a friend. I hated being at odds with her.

"Hi, Kate. It's good to hear from you."

Silence. I waited.

"Harry, I have more bad news." *So, no make up. Damn.*

"What's happened?"

"Charlie Maxwell is dead. Looks like suicide. I'm at her home. You want to come on over?"

Oh, hell. Not another.

"Geez, Kate. Okay, I'll be there in..." I looked at my watch. "Twenty-five minutes."

I was there in twenty. A couple of police cruisers and an ambulance were parked outside the house. Lonnie Guest stood on the front porch, his hands in his pockets.

"Another one, Starke. Seems to me there are too many people dyin' around you, an' that's a fact. Glad I ain't your friend."

"Me too, Lonnie. Me too."

I went inside and found Kate standing in the bathroom doorway. Doc Sheddon was already there, doing his thing.

"Well, it looks like he decided to get comfortable before he cut his wrist," Doc said. "A nice bath, scented candles, a bottle of red..."

"Wait a minute," I said. They both turned to look at me. "He? What do you mean, he? I thought you said it was Charlie Maxwell."

"See for yourself," Kate said. She wasn't smiling. She was

deadly serious. She backed out of the doorway so that I could enter.

Charlie Maxwell was lying naked in a bath full of pink water. Her left arm was hanging over the side. There was a gash in her left wrist maybe six inches long, and deep, almost to the bone. There was some arterial blood splashed on the walls and ceiling, but most of it had drained onto the floor beside the bath, forming a pool that stretched almost to the door. I stepped in, sidestepped to avoid the blood, and approached the foot of the tub. She was as white as a sheet of paper, a stark contrast to the dark brown hair; the fact that it was wet made it even more startling. Her breasts, smaller than I thought, were just above the water line. She was still quite beautiful, in a strange sort of way. I looked down, and there it was, visible even through the pink water. She was a man, all right.

But that wasn't all. I noticed something else.

"It wasn't suicide, Kate. It was murder."

"What? Why do you say that?"

"She was left-handed. The cut is on her left wrist. There's no way she did that to herself."

Kate looked at Charlie's arm, then at me. "Are you sure?"

"Oh yeah. I had coffee with her, remember?" The look I got should have shriveled me.

"I remember." Her voice was cold.

"She used a French press, and she not only poured with her left hand, she held her cup with it, too. She was murdered."

Kate looked at Doc. He shrugged. "I'll know more when I get her—*him*, on the table. Time of death is hard to tell because of the water, but at least ten hours, late yesterday evening, I should think."

"Shit," Kate snarled. "So this is a damn crime scene, and we've compromised it. Come on, Starke. Let's get out of here."

She hadn't called me Starke in more than five years.

"*Guest*," she yelled as she slowly stepped out onto the front port. "Get this place taped off. I need to get the crime scene techs here."

"What the hell for? She topped herself, didn't she?"

Kate glared at him. "Tape it off, Sergeant. Now. I'll get some backup. In the meantime, try to keep the lookers away. Keep them back on the road. There's already been too much foot traffic inside the house, and probably around it, too."

She radioed in and made the requests for the techs and extra officers, and then she turned to me.

"Spill it, Harry." Her face was serious.

"Spill what?"

"I want to know everything that you know about her.... Him."

"Kate, I don't know a whole lot more than I told you on Saturday. I was following up with my investigation for Willard. I needed to interview her about Tabitha. I only met her twice; once at the Read House for coffee, and the other time right here. I told you. She called me; she thought she was being stalked. I nixed that idea. Maybe I was wrong; maybe she was. When I left her, she was in good spirits, great spirits."

"Yeah. I'm sure she was."

"Cut the sarcasm, Kate." I was becoming angry. "I told you everything that happened that day, and I haven't seen or heard from her since."

She nodded.

"There's something else," I said. "Tabitha had a room

here. She stayed with Charlie when she wasn't up on the mountain. I meant to take a look at it while I was here on Saturday but somehow... well, it slipped my mind."

"Yeah, I bet it did."

"Dammit, Kate. Get off my back, will you?"

"Okay, okay, but there's nothing we can do now, not until the scene has been processed. You said she thought she was being stalked, tell me about that?" Her continued use of 'she' was understandable. Charlie had been a very beautiful woman.

"She thought someone was following her. She said she saw him three times. She thought he was white, but that's debatable. He was covered up, so he might have been black. He was tall, well built. That's all she could tell me. She saw him when she left me at the Read House, and again the next day at the gym in the new mall." Kate looked at me, her eyes wide. I nodded, and continued, "She saw him a third time on Friday, at Angelique, the clothing store, also in the mall. Kate, I thought it must have been Duvon James, and that he was shadowing me. I'd already caught him following me in Tree's BMW. It made sense. At that time, I'd had two run-ins with Tree. Now, though... after this... hell, I just don't know."

"You didn't see the man, right?"

"No."

She stared at me. It wasn't nice. It made me feel itchy, like something was crawling up my back. I didn't like it. It lasted but a minute, and then she shrugged and turned away.

"One more thing," I called after her as she walked away. "Charlie's laptop. I noticed it wasn't on the coffee table where it had been that Saturday I came here to see her. Maybe she moved it."

Kate nodded. "I'll look for it when I can get back in there."

"You'll look for it? Does that mean you're going to leave me out of this?"

"Have to, Harry. You're a person of interest in this one, too. You knew her. You've been here at her house, and God only knows what else. Oh, and I'm also going to want to know where you were last night, but I'll do that later. Think about it. For now, you're outta here."

She turned her back on me and walked back toward the house.

Geez. What did she mean by 'Think about it?'

28

One of the first things I do when I get into the office on Monday mornings is check my e-mail. It's not something I usually do over the weekend. I try to keep a little time for myself. This weekend, with all that had happened, was no exception.

As usual, there were dozens of them. Most were just junk. I was almost done deleting them, and about to click the garbage can to send a message from someone I didn't recognize to eternity, when something stopped me. Only rarely do I open e-mails from senders I don't know. Tim has hammered home the dangers so often it's gotten beyond irritating, but there was something about one sender's address that caught my attention. CM2621@nycpit.com. CM? Charlie Maxwell? I hesitated, and then took the plunge and opened it. It was from her. Date and time stamped 6:17 p.m., 1/31/2015. It must have been sent just before she was killed.

The message was three words, no more. *Check it out.* Check what out? Then I saw the attachment. I opened it. It was a single photograph, a picture of a dog. Her dog. Why would she send *that* to me? I only saw the animal once. I couldn't even remember the mutt's name. *Buster, was it?*

I shrugged, but forwarded the e-mail to Tim with a message to look at it and then see me. Then I had Jacque call everyone into the conference room.

"Okay, folks. It's crunch time. I have three dead bodies, Falk, Olivia Hansen, and Charlie Maxwell; four if you count Tabitha Willard. I'm a person of interest in the Hansen killing, and probably in Charlie Maxwell's too, and I don't like it. It could get out of hand. It's time to do something or get off the pot. I need something to work with, and I need it now. So what have we got?"

They all looked at me, horrified.

I'd been keeping everyone up to speed with the investigation, so they already knew about Falk and Olivia. They had all seen me dragged out of the office for questioning, but they didn't know about Charlie.

"Charlie Maxwell is dead?" Bob looked at me expectantly.

I told them what I knew, which at that point wasn't much, other than it was murder made to look like suicide, and that she was a he. That got their attention, but I needed to move on.

"You have what I have, people, but it all directly effects what we are doing. At least I think it does. So..." I looked around the room. "Ronnie. Let's start with you. What have found out about Harper's Foundation?"

"Quite a bit. It's murky, and we can prove very little, but by conjecture—"

"Conjecture isn't going to get it, Ronnie. I need facts. Hard facts."

"I wish I had 'em, but I don't. Harper and his team are good, very good, and they've woven a seriously muddy web of offshore companies, shell corporations, and bank accounts. Some of them are buried four and five layers deep. I've seen some devious schemes in my career, but this one is designed to hide assets, mystify, and confuse on a grand scale. Harry, conjecture is all we have, and maybe all we'll ever have unless we can dig into their actual, official finances, and I don't see that happening. Ever."

"Well damn," I said. "What *do* you have?"

Ronnie looked across the table at Mike, then at me, cleared his throat, and said, "It's a nightmare, Harry. It's a spider's web of shell, shelf and offshore companies. There are accounts in Dubai, the Caymans, Bermuda, the Bahamas, and probably elsewhere too."

He flipped the screen on his iPad, looked up at me, and said, "Dubai seems to be the hub of the foundation's activity. It's well known for its emphasis on business and trade for a number of reasons. One is its close geographical proximity to Iran and other Middle Eastern regimes that are under close scrutiny by the Office of Foreign Asset Control, the OFAC. The fact that Dubai has no taxes and that there's total freedom to move funds in and out of the country is another. A third is their attitude toward secrecy in banking. Dubai has a long-held tradition of 'ask no questions.' Their approach to commercial and financial regulations, and especially toward foreign financial crimes, has attracted big money from around the world, much of it in cash or gold."

"How does that effect the foundation?" I asked.

"I'm coming to that. Dubai's financial posture provides cover for a non-profit like Harper's to operate under the radar. With all of the international banks, money exchange houses, and trading companies to monitor, the OFAC, which is tasked with imposing sanctions on rogue countries, entities, and individuals, simply doesn't have the resources to monitor the foundation and the complex structure that we think is funding his efforts in the U.S. financial system."

"Geez, Ronnie. We never have these conversations without you giving me a headache. Go on."

He grinned. "That's what you pay me for, boss. Anyway, let's take a quick look at the foundation itself.

"The initial funding came from a sweet real estate investment Old Man Harper, Little Billy's granddad, made in Dubai a few years before he died. He borrowed $735,000 against one of his life insurance policies—which cannot be traced by the way—and thus he was able to buy and sell real property all across the Emirates. When the markets exploded, he made a killing with his access to insider information. As his investments grew, he recognized the need to shield the money and block all transparency, so he used the money from his investments to start the William G. Harper Foundation."

He grinned widely at me and Mike, then continued.

"As it turned out, the Harper Foundation also came in handy as a place to receive political donations from countries, entities, and individuals that wanted to leverage his influence—bribe him, in other words. Over the years, that initial $735,000 loan has grown into a sum of money capable of exerting considerable influence." He paused and took a deep breath.

"Now for the interesting part. When Harper the younger, Little Billy, took over the running of the Harper Foundation, he too realized its potential. His biggest challenge, however, was to devise a scheme to get the funds back into America. With it being registered in Dubai, and with him being a senior elected official, he couldn't structure the funds through the banking system due to the heightened regulations and oversight created by the Dodd-Frank legislation. So the Harper Foundation created a limited partnership to manage the investments."

"And that would be Jesper Hogstrum of Geneva, right?" I said.

He nodded. "Hogstrum is, as you know, a lawyer. He was made the general partner, the Harper Foundation itself being the limited partnership with 99.9% ownership. With more than $800 million in capital, the Harper Foundation is able to make plenty of legitimate investments in hedge funds, private equities, commodities, blue chip stocks, and so on. There are also ample funds to invest in other, albeit illegal, projects that would also benefit him. Interest, dividends, return of capital from the limited partnership to the foundation to make more legitimate charitable contributions; all provided additional cover for his shady activities. Still with me?"

"No," I said, "but go on."

"There's not much more but, as I said, it's almost all conjecture. So, we come now to Nickajack Investments and the other shell companies. There are a great many more than the three we're interested in. Investments into those companies could take the form of loans or equity. Since they're registered offshore, it's impossible to track money flow or ownership. Harper can use those shell companies and others like them to make contributions, take out loans, and compensate himself and others, none of it traceable. He has, in fact, created the proverbial cash cow."

"Done?" I looked at him.

He nodded. I had a headache.

"Mike. Anything to add?"

He shook his head. I could tell by the mystified look on his face that he'd had almost as much trouble following the narrative as I had.

"That was way too much information to digest all at once. Can you put it down on paper for me, Ronnie? Something I can study."

"Already have. You'll find an e-mail in your inbox with a file attached. You can open it in your iPad."

"Thanks. I'll spend some time on it when we're finished here. By the way, Tim, speaking of e-mails, I forwarded one to you, from Charlie Maxwell. It has an attachment, a photo. She told me to check it out, but I could make no sense of it. See if you can figure it out and let me know if you find anything."

Tim made a couple of notes, and then said, "I'll take a look at it as soon as we're done here."

"Okay, so what have you been able to find out about the pendant?"

"Not much. There are thousands of pictures on the web of jewelry with similar designs, and lots of references to snakes and serpents, most of it relating to the Hindu religion, but that's about it. Nothing specific."

I said, "Well, I've been able to find out quite a lot about it. You're right. It does have its origins in Hinduism, but what we have here is something quite different."

For the next fifteen minutes, I related what I now knew about the pendant and how I thought it might fit into the investigation, leaving out my encounters with Olivia Hansen and Senator Michaels, of course. Fortunately, they didn't question me how I'd found out as much as I had, thank God.

How the hell I would have managed to explain that, I had no idea.

Well, now at least we knew something. How it all tied in to the big picture was something else again. It was time for some direct action.

"Bob. I need to find out who's been following me, and maybe Charlie Maxwell, too. Someone's been tailing me in a silver Honda CRV, late model. He could be black, but he could also be white; Charlie just wasn't sure. If he was black, it could be Duvon James; I believe he's been following me in Tree's BMW. If so, why the Honda? Charlie Maxwell spotted him, the same person—at least she thought it was the same person—three times. On two of those occasions, it could well have been Duvon because of where she spotted him, outside the Green Tree Mall. The third time, she saw someone outside the Read House. That was on the afternoon I first met her. He was on foot then, but the CRV could have been parked in the multi-story just down the street. We have to find him. I've spotted the Honda three times, the last time on Sunday morning outside the Read House. I tried to catch him, but he was too quick. By the time I got turned around, he was gone.

"So, Bob, I want you to find him. I also want you to organize some surveillance. I need tails put on Tree, Duvon and... I think Harper."

"That's a bit risky, don't you think?"

"Maybe, but after what we've learned here today, I think it's worth it. Whoever you hire to do the job, make sure they're discreet. If Harper finds out, there'll be all hell to pay."

I ended the meeting and went back to my office. I needed a drink. I looked at my watch. It was just after noon. Early, but what the hell. I took the bottle of scotch from my cabinet, poured myself a stiff one, took a sip, and relished the fire as it slid down my throat. Next I called Mike into the office and asked him to run to the Deli and get me a sandwich, and then I fired up my iPad and opened Ronnie's file. He was right. It was a big one.

The sandwich arrived less than ten minutes later, and I settled myself down in one of the leather armchairs and ate as I read. It was almost five o'clock when I finally came up for air. What I'd learned was incredible. Harper's empire stretched around the world: a dozen banks, more than sixty shell corporations, real estate, hedge funds, and so on, a vast network of shadowy enterprises with no substance that I could use. All good stuff, but without the actual financial information to go along with it, it wasn't a whole lot of help. Hell, I couldn't even tie Harper directly to any of it. I could suspect, but... Ronnie was right. It was all conjecture.

I hit the button and sent the file to the wireless printer. A sketch with the text outlined the structure of the Harper Foundation and its activities.

Interesting. All of that information must be kept somewhere, probably on Harper's computer. If not his, well... I guess it could be anywhere. Must look into that.

I was still at the office browsing Ronnie's file when Kate called. She didn't waste any time with small talk.

"You were right. There was no laptop. We also have the preliminary results from the autopsy. She had drugs in her system. Nothing dramatic: Rohypnol, Ruffies. Where were you on Saturday night, Harry?"

"Oh come on, Kate. You don't think for one minute that I drugged Charlie and then slit her wrist, do you?"

"No, but Guest does. Where were you? Do you have an alibi?"

"I was out. Investigating the pendant."

"By yourself?"

"No."

"Come on, Harry. Who were you with? It's important."

"Kate, I can't tell you. It would break a confidence."

"Oh my God. You were out with a woman. You're damn addicted." And with that, she hung up.

I tried to call her back, but she wouldn't answer. Dammit.

29

It was just after eight o'clock on Tuesday morning when I dumped myself down on a stool in front of Tim's desk.

"Okay, Tim. What did you make of Charlie's e-mail? That photo means nothing to me. She's been dead more than forty-eight hours. Was she trying to tell me something?"

"Harry, it's pretty cool. Simple, but cool. I'm almost certain it's a Steganographic cipher generated by a simple computer program. The program performs monoalphabetic encryption, and decryption, using a keyword to create a 26-character cipher alphabet and then it hides a ciphertext within the pixels of a bit map image file—"

"Oh my God. Doesn't anybody speak English anymore?"

Tim grinned. "That is what your image is, Harry, a bitmap. It's pretty simple; a kid could do it. The thing is, though, simple or not, it will fool anyone who isn't computer savvy. No one would think of looking into the guts of a photograph for a message. It would also have to have been generated by someone who knows computers."

"Charlie was a systems analyst."

He smiled. "That would do it. So, all we need is a copy of the program, the keyword, and the image. I have the program. We have the image. Do you have the keyword?

"No. At least, not that I know of."

"I'd watch your inbox. That first e-mail with the image was pre-scheduled. I'd imagine there'll be another one coming. If not, we're screwed."

I called up my e-mail account. Just a half-dozen run-of-the-mill messages, most of them junk. Nothing more from Charlie. *Dammit.*

"Tell me more about this steno code, or whatever it is," I said. How does it work?"

"Harry, it's not easy to explain in a way you'll understand it."

"Give it a shot."

He took a deep breath. "You asked for it. Steganography allows us to conceal information inside a computer file. The file could be an image file, a photograph, as we have here, or it could be a doc file, even a program file. Image files are ideal. The steganographic coding is inserted into a transport layer, the photo. Your sender might choose an innocuous image file, a doggy pic, and adjust the color of every fiftieth pixel, or any other number, to correspond to a letter in the alphabet, a change so subtle that someone not actually looking for such a change wouldn't notice it.

"The advantage of steganography over an encrypted message, a code, is that the message does not attract attention to itself, as would an openly coded message. No matter how unbreakable such a coded message might be, it would be sure to attract attention, should it get into the wrong hands. Cryptography is used to protect the contents of a message.

Steganography does much more than that. It conceals not only the content of a message, but also the message itself. Cool, huh?"

"Yeah. Cool. Very cool. She was smart, Charlie. Very smart."

"Well, smart or not, if she didn't send us the key we'll never be able to decipher it. We need the key, Harry."

I nodded. "It'll come. She wouldn't have gone to all that trouble and then leave out the key. I'll keep watching for it. I'll let you know as soon as I get it."

It came the next day, in the afternoon.

30

I'd been checking my e-mail account throughout the day. By three o'clock, there was still nothing, and I was getting antsy. Finally, at exactly three thirty, there it was. I didn't bother to open it. I forwarded it straight to Tim, then picked up the phone and buzzed him to let him know that it was in his inbox.

No sooner had I put the landline down than my cell phone buzzed. I looked at the screen. *Unknown caller*.

"This is Harry Starke."

"Harry, it's Linda Michaels. Can you talk, privately?"

I was instantly alert.

"Just a second. I'll close the office door... Okay, we can't be heard. What is it? You sound—"

"I am," she interrupted. "I'm pissed. Harry, I— that is *we* —have a problem. I had a visit from Congressman Harper today. It was not a pleasant visit. He wanted something, something I'm not prepared to give him."

I had a hollow feeling in the pit of my stomach. "And what would that be?"

"Votes, Harry. He wants me to endorse him in his run for the Senate. He knows I can deliver several key constituencies, the most important of which is the senior senator from Tennessee."

"So? That's not a problem. You either endorse him or you don't. It's your choice."

"Not quite, Harry. For one thing, I don't like the man. I have a bad feeling about him. I've had it for years. He throws his weight around the Capitol, demands favors, and... well, I don't think he's honest. It's not something I can put my finger on, just a gut feeling, but I've been in this business a long time, and my gut is rarely wrong. I told him I wouldn't do it."

"What did he say?"

"Not much. He put a photograph down on my desk in front of me. It was a photo of you and me, Harry. It was taken in the restaurant, nothing compromising other than that I was with you, and that's fine. We're both adults, both single, and we have no history together. We can do whatever the hell we like with our private lives. No, Harry, it was the way he smiled that bothered me. He simply got to his feet and said, 'I'm sure you'll want to reconsider, Senator.' That was it. No direct threats. He simply walked out of the room. Harry, what if there's more? What if there *was* a camera in that room? I have it swept regularly, but you know what goes on around here better than anyone."

Oh boy, do I ever.

"Okay, Linda. Here's what we're going to do. I need to talk to you. I'll leave for Washington as soon as I can."

"When, Harry? Chattanooga is not an easy place to travel from."

"It's not a problem. At least, I hope not. My father has a Lear. If his pilot is available, I can be out of here in a couple of hours. I need to call him. I'll do that, and then call you back. Give me your number."

After she gave me her cell phone number, I hung up and called my father.

"Dad, it's me."

"How are you, son?"

"Fine, Dad... Dad, I need a favor, a big one. It's urgent."

"What is it?"

"I need to get to Washington, in a hurry."

He was silent for a moment, and then said, "The Lear has full tanks. Joe is in the other office. Hold on a minute."

I could hear faint voices talking, and then he was back. "Harry, Joe is leaving for the airport right now. He should be there in fifteen minutes, no more than that. He has to file a flight plan, but he should be ready to take off in less than an hour... Is there anything you want to talk to me about, son?"

"Oh hell yeah, but not right now. I don't have time. I'll get with you when I get back. I may need some help. You up for it?"

"You got it. Take care, Harry."

I disconnected and called Linda.

"I leave Chattanooga in an hour. The flight takes about an hour and forty-five minutes, which should put me on the ground no later than..." I looked at my watch. It was almost four o'clock. "Let's say seven. Can you pick me up at the airport?"

"There'll be a car waiting for you at the VIP lounge. The driver will know where to go. His name is Grant."

"That'll do it. I'll see you in about three hours, give or take a few minutes."

"Thank you, Harry. I... I... appreciate it."

"You don't need to thank me, Senator. It's the least I can do."

I disconnected, grabbed some clean clothes from the office closet, and was on my way to the airport in less than thirty minutes. Joe was already warming up the Lear's engines.

We arrived in the Washington area right on time. Unfortunately, air traffic in the circuit was heavy, and we had to circle for fifteen minutes before we were allowed to land. The car was already waiting. I had Joe make sure the plane was refueled and ready to go at short notice. I also told him to grab a room at a nearby hotel, to keep his cell phone turned on, and wait for my call.

From the airport, it was a drive of just thirty minutes on U.S. 1, south of the Beltway, to a rather dowdy-looking house in a quiet cul-de-sac just off the main road. The driver dropped me at the front door, and I rang the bell. It was opened immediately by what could only have been a Secret Service agent.

"Mr. Starke?"

I nodded.

"ID please."

He glanced at it, nodded, and handed it back to me. "This way please, sir."

The house was much larger than it had seemed from the outside. He led me through the foyer, through what must be the living room, and into a large office, or maybe it was a library. She was seated by herself in front of a log fire, staring into the flames. The agent closed the door quietly behind him.

"Hello, Harry." She got up and gave me a peck on the cheek. "It's good to see you again. I wish it were under better circumstances. Sit down, won't you?"

She looked tired. She also looked lovely. She was wearing a white woolen dress, and her shoes lay on the floor beside her chair.

I sat. "It's good to see you again, too." I looked around the room. It was Old World Washington, D.C., high ceilings and wood paneling. "Where exactly are we, Senator?"

"Oh, Harry, please call me Linda. This," she tilted her head and smiled, "is a Secret Service safe house. It's at my disposal whenever I need it. Being Chairman of the Appropriations Committee has its benefits. Now, you've had time to think. What have you come up with?"

"Not a lot. Since you called I haven't been able to do anything else but think, but I need more information, Linda. You want to talk to me?"

"I wouldn't have dragged you up here if I didn't. But before I do, I want to say something."

I nodded. "Go on."

"You need to know, Harry, that I am an honest politician, and there are few enough of those around here. I cannot be bought. I will not be intimidated. I will not bow to coercion. I will not support Harper. If we can't put a stop to this, and if he really can ruin me, then by God he must do it, but I'll bring the son of a bitch down with me. Harry, if you're willing to help, I'm prepared to fight him and let the chips fall where they may."

I smiled at her. "Of course I'm willing, and we'll not be

alone. I already have several of my staff working on it, and my father's standing by; his resources are almost infinite."

She heaved a visible sigh of relief. "Good. Now your retainer."

"Please, Linda. Don't insult me."

She smiled, just a quick twitch of her lips. "Fine. What is it you want to know?"

"Well, you can start by telling me about Mystica. I need to know all about it. How it works. How many members. Who they are."

"All right."

"Wait just a minute. Do you mind if I record this?"

"I'd rather you didn't, but if you must, you must. I trust you, Harry. Don't let me down."

She waited while I set up my digital recorder. When I was done, I nodded.

"Where would you like me to begin?" she asked.

"Let's start with the membership. How many members are there?

"I don't know, but I think there must be quite a lot, and I say that because of the number of people I've seen in the gym, the restaurant, and the clothing stores wearing pendants."

"Did you recognize any of them?"

She looked at me, unsure, and then nodded slowly. "I've seen one other senator and two congressmen at the mall and in the restaurant—one congressman was a woman, the other a man. They didn't see me. As soon as I spotted them, I left."

"How about their names, Linda."

She hesitated, but said, "Senator Jordan Wickham, Congresswoman Glenda Webster, and Congressman Henry Studdington."

"How many times did you see them?"

"Just once, each on different occasions. They were not alone. They may have been guests of other members."

"And that's all? Did you ever see anyone else there that you knew?"

"No." She shook her head.

"What about Harper? Did you ever see him there?"

"No. Never."

"Linda, Harper wears a gold ring on his left pinky finger. Have you seen it?"

"I've seen it, but I've never looked at it. Why do you ask?"

"It has a replica of the pendant on it."

She looked stunned, then, quietly said, "So he's a member, then."

"Possibly. It's too coincidental, but I don't know for sure." I mulled it over, but nothing came. I shook my head.

"Now... Linda. Please tell me exactly how and why you became involved."

She lowered her head. "My husband, Tom, died more than ten years ago. I loved him very much, and when he passed, I was very much alone and—so I thought at the time—very vulnerable. I was a junior senator then."

She looked up at me; there were tears in her eyes.

"I had needs, Harry. I still do, but with the position I was in... Well, I felt I could trust no one. I was on the fast track in the party and, well, you know how Washington is, so I kept myself to myself. I didn't, *wouldn't,* accept invitations from men. I didn't dare. The publicity... Then, one day, my secretary walked into my office and caught me, well, you know. She was very sympathetic, understanding. We talked. She asked. She understood. No, Harry. I'm not a lesbian. You of all people should know that. And neither is she, although she was in the same situation that I was, but she had found OM."

I nodded. "I've heard of that. I know what it is."

She nodded. "Anyway, Heather was discreet, and one night we went out together and she took me to her... nest, I suppose you'd call it, and that was it. I liked it. It filled my needs, at least for a while, and no one knew who or what I was, or cared.

"And then, one day, while I was in the middle of a session, the practitioner, a man called Terry, I think his name was, asked if I was happy with the service. I told him I was, but there must have been something in my voice that told him different, because he said, 'There's another level of OM, you know.' Well I didn't, but he could tell I was interested, and he told me about Mystica. In detail. He said it was similar to OM, but came with more... more... benefits. The more he told me, the more intrigued I became, and he knew it."

"Had you ever met this Terry before?"

"Hmm, maybe. As a practitioner, he was new to me, but I think I'd seen him there at least once before."

I nodded.

"Anyway, he told me that Mystica was based in Chattanooga. He gave me a business card with a name and phone number on it, and he gave me my pendant. He said I could call the number on the card and they would arrange things. He also assured me that I had nothing to worry about. Mystica was a very discreet and very exclusive club. He asked for nothing in return.

"I kept the pendant and the card for almost six months before I did anything about it. Then I called the number. A man answered the phone, told me his name was Lester, and he gave me some instructions."

Aha! That would be Shady. Now I know his connection.

"He told me there was no membership fee, but that I would be required to pay for the room. I could take it on an as-needed basis, or I could lease it outright. I chose to lease it. He said he would send me a key to the building, a keycard for the room, and directions for how to find the place—there's another door at the back. He also explained how the pendant worked, and he promised me complete anonymity. The suite is expensive, but the rate included maid service, and I could afford it. I did not, however, believe the anonymity promise."

And there it was, the answer to the key and the business card in Tabitha's clutch. At least I hoped it was.

"Linda, those pendants are exclusive. They are only handed out by founding members of Mystica. If this Terry person gave one to you, it must have come from someone else. I think you were targeted, possibly because of who and what you are."

"In retrospect, I'm sure you're right." She shook her head, exasperated. "My package arrived the next day by FedEx. I flew to Chattanooga two days later, booked in at the Read House, rented a car, and drove to the mall. I parked at the rear, found the door, and checked out my suite. I have to tell you, Harry: I was impressed."

"Did you ever meet this Lester character?"

"No. My instructions were to leave a check on the washstand in the bathroom. I, of course, always left cash, in an envelope. Anyway, I didn't stay that first day. I went back to the Read House and the following day, I had the Secret

Service thoroughly sweep the place for bugs, cameras and so on. They declared the suite clean, and I was all set."

"Linda, how many suites are there, do you know?"

"Not really. Ten, maybe twelve, and there are at least six cubicles used by the OM practitioners."

So that's where Tabitha worked.

"Anyway, the next day, I booked a table in the restaurant —oh, and I joined the gym too—and I had dinner. The first night, nothing, nor the second, nor the third, but on the fourth night, well, you know the rest of the story, and that, Harry, was the only time I ever played the game, except for you, that is, and oh how glad I am that I did play the game with you."

"Me, too, Linda."

"I told you that I had taken only one other man up to the suite; that was the one. I wasn't too bothered with who might see me in the restaurant, but I still didn't trust the security inside the suite, so I kept the lights off as much as possible, and I kept the talk to a minimum... So there could have been no photographs. Audio, perhaps, but I doubt it. With you, however...

"Anyway, nothing happened. The guy was a jerk and I got rid of him, quickly, but it made no difference to the way I felt. I was disgusted with myself. I felt like a hooker. I swore I'd never do it again. But I did use their OM service a few times, to relieve stress. Hell, that's not true either. I enjoyed it... and then you came along."

I grinned at her. "Go on."

"Harry, with you it was different." There were tears in her eyes. "I don't know what came over me. You were so... I wanted it all. I wanted to see you, for you to see me, to touch me. I wanted to hear the things you said to me. I..."

I went over to her, knelt down beside her. The tears were rolling down her cheeks; she was crying gently.

"Shhh. It's all right. I wanted those things, too."

Abruptly, she gathered herself together, pushed me away, sat up straight, cleared her throat, turned toward me, and said, "Enough, Harry. That was inappropriate of me. I'm a senator, for God's sake. I can handle this."

"Senators are human, too," I said.

"Humph. Not this one." It was said with a smile, but I knew that deep down she meant it.

"Do you want to continue?"

There was steel in her eyes when she looked at me. "Of course I do. What's next?"

"I need to get back to Chattanooga. I want to check out a couple of things. Tabitha Willard had a key in her purse, and a business card. I also know who your man Lester is. His name is Lester Tree, known as Shady. He runs the mall. Has an office at the end of the block. He's a real piece of work. I think he may be in bed with Harper. With what you've told me tonight, and with what I already have, I might be able to make the connection. We'll see."

I looked at my watch, and saw that it was after eleven.

"You can stay with me tonight, but I have an early appointment in the Senate tomorrow morning, so I'll need to leave here by seven."

"You sure?"

"Of course. Grant will take you to the airport. I'll let him know."

She got up, took my hand, and led me to the stairs. Fifteen minutes later, I was in heaven again.

31

I landed in Chattanooga late the next morning. I went straight to the office, showered, changed clothes, and headed out again. I needed to do something and it wouldn't wait.

I drove to the mall and circled the block to make sure there was no one around, then parked at the rear close to the wall, and then sat there for several minutes, just to make sure I was alone.

The door I was looking for was in the center of the block. It wasn't marked in any way, just an ordinary steel door painted a dull, battleship gray with a lock and a D-shaped handle.

Sure that I wasn't being watched, I got out of the car, locked it, and walked quickly to the door. I inserted Tabitha's key into the lock. It fit. I turned it. The lock clicked. I pulled the door open and found myself in the passageway behind the restaurant.

All right. That's one question answered. Now we know what part Tabitha played in this mess.

I didn't need to go any further. I backed out of the doorway and pulled the door shut behind me. I was about to turn around to walk back to my car when something cold and hard touched the back of my neck.

"Freeze, Starke. Don't turn around. I have a message for you... Keep your nose out of what don't concern you. Drop your investigation of Mystica. If you don't, you'll end up in the river."

I was about to speak when... *BAM*. My head seemed to explode in a flash of brilliant white light, and then everything went black.

I woke up with a splitting headache, and no idea how long I'd been out. I was propped up against the rear wall of the mall. My head hurt like hell.

I reached inside my jacket. The M&P9 was gone. *Dammit.* My watch was gone, too. *Dammit!* I felt in my jacket pocket for my phone. *Dammit again!* My car keys? *Damn!* Wallet? It should be in my front pants pocket. Okay. Got it. Thank God for small mercies. My car was still there, too. No keys, not good, right? Don't bet on it. I kicked the bumper, hard, set off the alarm, and then sat on the hood to wait for the cops. Why is it that there's never one around when you need one?

I didn't have to wait long. Someone must have called it in because a cruiser soon rolled by. I waved it down and asked the officer to call Kate. I also reported the attack and the theft of my gun.

Kate arrived almost an hour later with the spare key to the Maxima.

"Here." She tossed it to me. "How many more times, Harry? One of these days I'm gonna be shoving you into a body bag. What was it about this time?"

"Same old, same old; just working the case, following a lead. I must have stepped on someone's toe. This was a warning. I was told to drop it or else."

"Okay, so what do you have for me?"

"Nothing concrete just yet," I lied. "I need a few more days, and then I think I'm going to need your help."

She looked at me through narrowed eyes. "Don't hang me out to dry, Harry. You understand?"

I nodded. She nodded, and then she turned, got back in her car, and drove away on McCallie, heading downtown. Not a word of goodbye, kiss my ass, nothing. She *was* still pissed.

32

Bob walked into my office just before ten the next morning, a big smile on his face. He was about to say something when he saw my face. I grinned up at him from my leather throne.

"Looks nasty, huh?" The welt on the side of my head had already turned blue. "It's not quite as bad as it looks, but I do have one hell of a headache."

I spent the next couple of minutes explaining what had happened, and what I had learned so far. When I finished, I asked him what he wanted.

He perked up. "Here you go, Harry. Here's your man. This is the guy who's been tailing you." He placed an eight by ten photo in front of me.

It was grainy, taken at night and through a car window, but he was recognizable. Just. I looked hard at the image. The ball cap was pulled down over his eyes, but I could tell he was white, and there was something familiar about the face.

"Bob, I think I've seen this guy somewhere. I can't quite

remember, but... How did you find him? Who did you hire for the tail?"

"This one I decided to do myself. Come on, Harry. It's what we do, right? I figured that if you were being followed, all I had to do was follow you, too. It took a little time. The guy knows what he's doing. He's not an amateur. I spotted him once, lost him almost immediately. Finally, I spotted him again on Lakeshore Lane." He grinned at the look I gave him. "That's right, Harry, right on your street."

"We need to find out who he is, Bob. See what you can do." I handed him the photo. "Make me a copy of that and let me have it back. Maybe something will come to me."

"I already have a copy." He put the print down on my desk.

"Okay, so what about Tree and his people—and Harper?'

"I hired a couple of ladies I've used in the past. You know them. Heidi and Selina?"

I nodded. I knew both of them well. Both were pros, free-lancers, though they worked mostly for one of my competitors. I wish I had room for them here, but I don't.

"Heidi stuck to Tree, but he left his office only to go home. The two soldiers never left his side. Harper was much the same. He was in his office all day, every day, and then at home each evening, except for last night when he had dinner at La Maison Ducat." He smiled at me. "He left Ducat around ten thirty and headed home. That's about it."

"Hmmm. So he knows Ducat, eh? I thought he might. He wears a ring with the pendant motif on it. I wonder... Is he a member of Mystica, or is he running it?"

Bob shrugged. "We'll never know unless somebody talks, or unless he does, and I don't see either happening anytime soon."

He was right. Linda didn't know. She hadn't seen him there. She hadn't even noticed his ring. Olivia Hansen didn't mention Harper, and now I couldn't go back and ask her, either. Likewise with Charlie Maxwell. *I wonder... what about Senator Wickham, Congresswoman Webster, and Congressman Studdington? Hmmm, it's a thought. Maybe later, if I can't figure it out some other way.*

"Any ideas, Bob?"

"Nope, other than coming right out and asking him."

That brought a smile to my face. *Now there's a thought, but then... what the hell?* Shock and awe is, after all, my preferred method of obtaining information. I figured it might be worth a try, but how?

After Bob left, I slammed through some much-needed paperwork—'much-needed' according to Jacque—but my heart wasn't in it. I looked at my watch. Noon. Linda would still be tied up in the senate, so I couldn't call her. *Dammit.*

I went out to lunch by myself, at the Deli, ate a sandwich, and then returned to the office. When I finally flopped down in my chair, it was just after two o'clock.

Idly, almost without thinking about it, I picked up the 8x10 Bob had taken of my tail. Something had been nagging me, something at the back of my mind. I was sure I knew this guy. I stared at it, put it down, picked it up again—and then it hit me, and I smiled to myself. *Got you, you bastard.*

33

I called my players into work the next day. It was Saturday, and I was well aware that it was an imposition, but it couldn't be helped. We had to figure out what the next play would be. I was now almost certain that Harper was the key to both Mystica and the three killings. How I was going to prove it was another matter. I was hoping Charlie's e-mails would cast a little light on the subject.

Jacque, Bob, Ronnie, Tim, Mike and I met in the conference room. I'd thought about inviting Kate, but nixed the idea. At this point, I really didn't have any reason to. Besides, I was still in the doghouse, and a person of interest in the Hansen killing. And she never did call back to get my alibi for the night Charlie was murdered.

Charlie's second e-mail had arrived late Thursday afternoon. I'd forwarded it to Tim but hadn't heard back from him. God help us if it was all a stupid ruse.

It wasn't.

We sat down together around the table. At the far end of

it, someone had set up a white dry-erase board. Tim had taken the seat in front of it and sat patiently sipping a large black coffee.

"Okay, people," I said, rubbing my hands together. "It's crunch time. What do we have? Tim, was that e-mail from Charlie Maxwell what you needed?"

"It was. It contained the key to the photo, which was easy enough to figure out once I had it. The photo contained three pieces of information: the name of a secret Dropbox account, and the username and password for it. The Dropbox had two Microsoft Excel files and a Word file.

"The word file was a letter from Charlie to you, Mr. Starke." He handed it to me. It was short and only took a couple of minutes to read.

Dear Harry,

If you are reading this note, I have truly screwed up, and I am probably dead. I planned it so that the two files you now have in your possession would be my insurance, my safety net if things went wrong. The files are the keys to all of Congressman Harper's financial dealings. He is, to put it bluntly, a crook. The files were given to me by Tabitha, who got them from Michael. You already know what happened to them. My idea was to e-mail them to you, delayed delivery. The first was scheduled to arrive in two days, the second, two days after the first. I could stop them and reschedule them anytime I wanted to, unless of course something happened to me. Obviously it did. Good hunting, Harry Starke. We could have had good times together, you and I.

Love,

Charlie

I looked up. They were all staring at me. I couldn't speak. I folded the note and put it in the inside pocket of my jacket. It wasn't something I wanted to share, at least not then. Tim, I knew would have read it, but I also knew he wouldn't have shared it. We would keep Charlie Maxwell's confidence... until it might be needed as evidence.

"What else, Tim? Tell me about the files."

"The first one is a list of names, complete with personal details. I'm pretty sure it's a list of members and potential members of Mystica. Some are starred; some have question marks beside their names. Harry, Olivia, and George Hansen are on the list, and so is—"

"Senator Michaels?"

He nodded.

"Damn, that alone could embarrass her."

"I don't think so, Harry. The list also includes eleven congressmen and five more senators. I have a feeling that the Feds will lock it away; I don't think they'll allow the government to be compromised by what really amounts to nothing more than a few minor sexual distractions."

"Okay, what about the other file?"

"Ronnie," Tim said, "this is your field. You tell him."

"The big one is actually a sort of balance sheet—no, it's more of a worksheet. A company's balance sheet reports the dollar amounts of a company's assets, liabilities, and owner's equity, or stockholders' equity, as of a predetermined date. This one is dated Wednesday, January fourteenth, twenty-four days ago, which is two days before Michael Falk was killed. Significant, right?"

No one answered.

"All righty then. I shall continue. Assets listed on a for-profit balance sheet usually include cash, accounts receivable, inventory, investments, land, buildings, equipment, some intangible assets, and anything else of value that the company might own. This type of balance sheet is prepared for use by management as a tool, and also for use by stockholders, generally as part of the company's annual report. It will list liabilities as well as assets, including loans payable, accounts payable, warranty obligations, taxes payable, and the list goes on. The balance sheet allows us to easily determine a company's working capital, and whether or not it is highly leveraged.

"A nonprofit foundation's balance sheet reports the dollar amounts of its assets, liabilities, and fund balances, or what most people refer to as its equity. The foundation can use the income generated from its assets to make legitimate charitable contributions and investments. Taxes are paid where they are required and everything's aboveboard. This type of balance sheet is available and open to public scrutiny.

"The one we have here, this... worksheet, is slightly different." Again, Ronnie looked around the table. "Questions, anybody?"

"Okay, smart ass," I said. "I'll bite. How is it different?"

Ronnie grinned. "This worksheet is, in fact, a second set of books for the Harper Foundation and Harper's financial dealings, and only available to Harper himself, and maybe a couple of select cronies. There are no liabilities listed, only assets, and they are huge, solely funded by unrestricted fund balances. As the controller of the fund, Harper has vast amounts of cash and assets at his disposal, all available for him to use to exert his influence. There are no checks and balances to prevent him from doing whatever he wants.

"Harper is into all sorts of shady dealings: blackmail, extortion, money laundering, influence peddling, you name it, it's all documented here. The Harper Foundation is just the beginning of Harper's financial empire; it's where the huge amounts of cash needed to fund his other less transparent projects, his 'investments,' are generated. Still with me?"

"Uh-huh. Go on."

"The cash is generated mostly through influence peddling. Donations are made to the Harper Foundation by for profit entities: defense contractors, foreign powers, companies in financial trouble looking for a helping hand, even individuals. In return, they get something they want from Congress, usually in the form of lucrative contracts, government-backed loans, or large grants. For instance, in October of 2014, WorldWide Solar made a donation to the Harper Foundation of $1.5 million. Three weeks later, they received a contract from the government worth an estimated $110 million. I have documented at least fifteen such instances over the past eighteen months of potential quid pro quo involving the Harper Foundation. Donations total more than $41 million. Government contracts and grants awarded soon thereafter total more than a billion dollars, and I'm finding more by the day."

He paused and took a drink of water. *Hell I need a drink, too, and not water.*

"All of his shady deals are listed here in this worksheet. The Harper Foundation's investments are in the public record, but the money, once it's invested, disappears into a multiverse of shell and offshore companies, including companies like Nickajack and Goodwin. Harper is then able to take out loans from those companies; essentially, he borrows his own money and he doesn't have to pay it back. Loans are not taxable income. According to this worksheet, he's taken out hundreds of such loans totaling hundreds of millions of dollars, most of them for small amounts, some not so small... That's about it."

"That's all good stuff, Ronnie, but can we tie it to Harper? If we can't, it's useless. Well, not exactly, but you get my meaning. I need hard evidence. If that's Harper's crooked financial empire, we need to be able to prove it... What? What are you laughing at?"

"You have the proof. It's in the file itself. The metadata."

"Metadata? I thought that was for photographs."

"It is, but metadata is also used for all sorts of other types of files, including Word files and... Excel files."

I stared hard at him. "Keep talking."

"So, all Excel files contain information other than that for which the file was created. It's hidden from general view as metadata, unless some wiz deletes it, but that didn't happen here. Most operators, and when I say most, I'm talking about people like you, Harry, and Jacque, Bob, Mike. Most people don't even know such metadata is present. Accountants, auditors and so on *are* familiar with it, but they bother with it only in rare circumstances. Metadata is the realm of the IRS, IT experts, and analysts. It incorporates a wealth of information about the given file, including the author's name, the date when the file was created and by whom, the date the file was last modified and by whom, and the date it was last saved. This can all be found within the file itself under the properties tag, but unless you know where to find it, it's not easy to access.

"And there's more. If you mouse over the file name in Windows Explorer, and then hit 'properties,' you get even more metadata. That'll include everything I've already mentioned, plus show the name and e-mail address of the administrator—in this case Gordon Harper.

"Harry, all of this is hard evidence. It shows the originator *and* the authorized users. We now know not only exactly what it contains, but who put it there."

"Can metadata be changed?" Bob asked.

"Some of it can; some of it can't. Some of it can be wiped, too; some of it can't. The statistics tab that includes the date the file was created, when it was last modified, and by whom, can't be changed or wiped. The only way to get rid of that information is to save the file under a different name. That would create a whole new set of statistics and metadata, but that hasn't happened here."

"So, what we have is an Excel file with its metadata intact?" I asked.

He nodded. "The file was originally created on April 15, 2012, and was last saved on Wednesday, January 14, 2015. We have the author of the file, Jesper Hogstrum; the administrator, Gordon Harper, and one other authorized user, Jackson Hope."

So now I had it, so I thought. All I had to do now was to get Harper to commit.

I had the rest of the weekend to think it over.

Monday was going to be H Day.

34

I woke early on Monday morning. It had been raining for most of the night. By seven o'clock I was driving into the city in the middle of a downpour, a torrent the wipers could barely cope with. It was going to be a hell of a day.

I arrived at the office at seven thirty, the last one to arrive. Everyone was nervous. The word was out. But this was the day we would bring down one of the country's most prominent political figures; no wonder they were all tense.

"Okay, everyone," I said, as I breezed in. "Great to see you all so bright and early. Let's get some coffee and go over it one more time."

At eight thirty, I made the call.

"Congressman Harper. This is Harry Starke. I'd like to make an appointment to see you. It's urgent. Can we do it early this morning?"

"I don't want to see you, Starke. I told you before: I know nothing about what happened to Falk. That should be the end of it."

"I don't want to talk to you about Falk."

"Then what?"

"Not over the phone, Congressman. You know better than that. Let's just say that I have something of interest, something you *need* to know."

"There's nothing you can say that will interest me, Starke—"

"Are you sure?" I interrupted him. "Are you absolutely sure?" He didn't answer.

I have him.

"Five minutes," he said. "I'll give you five minutes. Not a damned second more, and it had better be good. Be here at... ten. If you're late, forget it." He slammed the phone down.

It was on. I called Kate and filled her in as best I could. Then I told her what I planned to do.

"I'm going in alone. I have a listening device. What? No, it's not a wire. It's a wristwatch, with video and audio transmission. I'm told the range is about a half mile. There's also a receiver unit with a digital recorder. I've tested it. It seems to work fine, and I've been assured that it will do the job." *And the Secret Service should know.*

"You'll know exactly what's going on in that office at all times."

"Harry. You can't do this. Harper isn't stupid. He's not going to give you what you want. If they are what you think they are, and they figure out what you're up to, you could wind up dead."

"You're right. It's not going to be easy. I'm going to have to jerk his chain a little. The receiver is small, about the size of a box of chocolates. It has a built-in speaker, but earbuds would work just as well. It records whatever it picks up onto a flash drive. The thing is, though, if everything works out the way I hope, we won't need it. What about it? Will you do it?"

"What do you mean, we won't need it?"

"I can't explain now. I don't have time. You'll just have to trust me, okay? Will you do it?"

"Oh, I trust you, all right." Was that sarcasm? "You'll go through with it anyway, no matter what I say."

"If not you, it'll have to be Bob and Tim. Bob is great, but police backup would be better. It'd make me feel better."

She paused. Then sighed. "What time?"

"I have to be there at ten. You'll need to drop by the office and pick up the gear. You'll also need to learn how it works, which shouldn't take more than a couple of minutes. Tim will handle that for you. Don't take any chances with the range of the thing. You should be as close to the Tower as you can. If you could find somewhere inside, that would be even better. I won't be able to hear you, but you should be able to hear and record everything."

"I'll be at your office in... twenty-five minutes."

"Great. Bob and Tim will be waiting for you. Talk to you later."

"Wait—be careful, Harry."

"Always am. Bye." I disconnected. I had to take a little time, compose myself.

I strapped the watch onto my left wrist. *I hope this thing works. If not, I'm going to be in a world of trouble.*

I slipped into my rig and put my jacket on over it, then retrieved my backup M&P9 from the safe. Once I'd satisfied myself that it was loaded, with one in the chamber, I slipped it into the holster under my arm. If I was frisked, it would be found, but I wasn't going to let anyone frisk me.

I entered the Tower a few minutes before ten, took the elevator to the top floor, and marched into Harper's office.

"He's waiting for you, Mr. Starke. You can go right in."

I nodded to the receptionist and pushed open the door. Harper was at his desk; Jackson Hope was at his. Harper had an enigmatic smile on his lips.

"Come on in, Starke. Frisk him, Jackson. See if he's carrying, or if he's wired."

Hope started to rise. I took a step sideways, toward the window. "Back off, Hope." He sat back down. "You know damn well I'm carrying. I always do. As for a wire, here, take a look." I opened my jacket and pulled my T-shirt all the way up to my neck, exposing my bare chest.

"Satisfied?" I had to think carefully now, about what I said next. No lies. I had to think like a politician. "Why would I be wired? You have this office bugged, camera and audio, I shouldn't wonder, right?"

He smiled but didn't answer. Hope, however, told me everything I needed to know. He glanced up at the bookshelf behind Harper's chair. I couldn't see it, but it was there all right. *I knew it! Now I have you, too, you cocky bastard.*

"Screw you, Starke. You have five minutes and the clock is running. Now get on with it. What the hell do you want?"

"I have you, Harper. I have the file."

"File? What the hell are you talking about?"

"I'm talking about the computer file that Michael Falk stole from you; the file that got him killed. It's the key to your entire corrupt financial empire. You know what it contains. That's why you had to get it back."

He didn't answer, but I could tell I'd hit a nerve.

"You used the Harper Foundation as your own personal piggy bank. You invested the foundation's legitimate assets into a web of phantom shell accounts, and then you took out loans from those companies; you borrowed your own money, the foundation's money, with no intention of ever paying it back. That's money laundering. You even paid dividends from those investments into the foundation, and then you churned that back into the quagmire in the form of more investments: another illegal act, more money laundering, with the foundation as the investor and you the only beneficiary. You used the funds to finance your political ambitions, and your extravagant lifestyle. It was a hell of a scheme, and it's all there, in the file."

"So you've got the file, so what? You can't tie me to it."

"Oh but I can. You know what metadata is, Harper?"

"Metadata? What the hell is metadata?"

"Will you tell him, Jackson, or will I?" I asked with a malicious smile.

Hope had gone white. He knew exactly what was coming.

"What's he talking about, Jackson?"

"Er..." Hope looked sick. "The files contain hidden data. Time stamps, the author, authorized users... the administrator."

Harper looked as if he'd been kicked by a mule. "Why are you doing this, Starke? Why are you poking your nose where it doesn't belong? What did I ever do to you?"

"Tabitha Willard. You made me cause her to die. I'll have to live with what she did for the rest of my life, and all because I was in the wrong place at the wrong time. I'll never forget the look on her face when she saw me, but it's also about justice, Congressman. It's all about justice, not only for Tabitha, but also for Michael Falk and Charlie Maxwell, and every other poor sucker that you've screwed over, and for poor Olivia Hansen. Why you had to kill her, I don't know—probably because of her connection to me. If so, I owe you for that one, too. You are guilty of a whole range of criminal activities, any one of which can and will put you away for the rest of your days, including conspiracy to commit murder, starting with Michael Falk."

"You can't prove any of that, you smartass piece of shit."

"No? You want to hear my theory? Maybe you'll change your mind."

"Screw you, Starke. Get the hell out of my office, and take your fantasies with you."

I smiled at him. He looked away.

"Here's what I think," I said. "Falk was killed because you caught him downloading your secret financial dealings from your computer. There's a camera up there in the bookshelf, isn't there?" I nodded toward the shelf behind his chair. "It records everything that goes on in this office. I suspected the office was monitored the first time I was here. You were so precise with your questions and answers, and with your dealings with my father's check. You made sure it was placed precisely on your desk so the camera could get a good view of it. It wasn't a huge leap to figure out the rest.

"Your man killed Falk, but then he found out that the drive was gone. You figured Tabitha must have it.

"You had Tree set his goons on Tabitha, scared her out of her wits. She gave up Charlie Maxwell, panicked, ran, then tossed herself off the bridge. Charlie was an unfortunate victim of circumstance. Her only sin was knowing Tabitha Willard.

"Your man killed Charlie." I looked at Hope as I said it. He stared back at me, unflinching. "He retrieved the drive and all was well. At least you thought it was. What you didn't know was that Charlie was an IT specialist. She downloaded the files, encrypted them, and sent them to me as an attachment to an e-mail. I have it all, Harper, every dirty deal you've ever done, every offshore account, every shell corporation, the loans, everything—and I know all about Mystica. I even have the file that contains the list of Mystica members. I'm sure some of them will be willing to talk, if only to keep their names out of the media."

"Your five minutes are up, Starke."

I smiled at him. "You had it all, didn't you, Congressman? More money than you could ever spend, but it wasn't enough. You needed more. You needed power. The sad thing is, you could probably have achieved it without taking the path that you did, but you're corrupt; you're rotten to the core, a truly evil man. You couldn't help yourself, so you resorted to blackmail and extortion, and you did it by exploiting your victim's most basic weaknesses, hence Mystica.

"Mystica was a tool designed to gather dirt on the rich and powerful, and it worked. But you made a mistake. Your arrogance let you down. You reached for the top, but you picked the wrong mark in Senator Linda Michaels."

"Michaels?" He smiled. "What if her little hobby was to become public, Starke? How about that?"

"Was that a threat, Congressman? If it was, it won't work. She just doesn't care. If she did, you would have gotten all you asked for. Then again, I don't think you have anything on her. She never really played the game, did she? That suite was just a place for her to get away from it all, a secure place to rest and relax. And one more thing. She had it swept for bugs and cameras on almost a weekly basis. She also had the lock changed."

I had him, and he knew it.

"She's incorruptible," I continued. "But Mystica? How, I asked myself, did she become a member? I knew from my conversations with Olivia Hansen, and she said very little, that the invitation to the club had to come from a founding member, not some kinky sex practitioner. Whoever it was that inducted her had to have gotten his instructions from such a member, and there is only one such member, isn't there, Congressman. You!"

He didn't answer.

"The first time I met you, I noticed that ring on your left hand. It was a dead giveaway. So I figured that the infamous Terry must work for you, but who was he? I couldn't figure it out, not until we set a trap to catch whoever was following me."

Harper said nothing. But he did push a button on the office intercom. Two seconds later, the door behind me squeaked. I stepped sideways, turning my back to the window so I could see the entire room. Hope started to rise, then sat back down. The door was opening slowly.

"Come on in, Terry. Don't be shy," I said quietly. The receptionist stepped into the room, gun in hand, suppressor attached.

"Nice weapon, Terry. Beretta, right?"

He turned to look at me, the gun low but aimed in my direction. His eyes were two chips of flint.

"Terry Hamlin," I said with a smile. "One-time First Lieutenant, dishonorably discharged, of the Army Rangers, now undercover black ops for the good congressman. You're older than you look, Terry. I've got to say, you took a bit of figuring out. We finally tracked you down when my investigator caught you following me. He managed to get a photo of you. Not a good one, but it sufficed. I knew as soon as I saw it that I'd seen you somewhere. It took me a while, but then it hit me. I'd seen your face a couple of times, sitting behind a computer, playing Little Billy's receptionist. Which you're not, is he, Congressman?"

No one answered, so I continued.

"Once I knew who you were, it was relatively simple to get hold of your records. You've been a very bad boy, Terry. That gun you're holding is going to put you away for the rest of your days— Little Billy here, too. They took a good slug out of young Falk's head. I'm sure they'll be able to make a match, and then it's goodbye, Terry, goodbye, Little Billy, goodbye, Jackson Hope."

"The hell you say," Hope snarled. I could see him out of the corner of my eye. "I didn't know about anything! I just do the books."

"Shut up, Hope," Harper growled.

"Screw you, Harper. I'm not going down for you. Starke, I—"

"Shut the hell up!"

Never for a moment did I turn my attention away from Hamlin. I watched his eyes. They narrowed. He was going to do it.

"Don't do it, Terry."

"Let him have it, Terry," Harper snarled.

Hamlin's gun began to move upward; his right eyelid lifted; his fingers twitched. Almost without thinking, I swept my right hand up under my jacket and, in one smooth movement, drew the nine. Without aiming, I fired. I'd practiced the move a thousand times. The bullet caught him low in the right shoulder. He staggered back several steps, eyes going to the small red spot with a surprised look on his face. He dropped to his knees, then sat back on his heels, hands hanging by his sides. The gun fell from his fingers. He looked up at me, stunned. I turned quickly toward Hope, but the man hadn't moved. Neither had Harper.

"I hope you got all that," I said into the watch.

I stepped forward and kicked Terry's gun away—it was indeed a Beretta—then moved back to the window. I took out my cell phone and hit 911. "Shots fired," I said, and gave the operator the address. I then turned my full attention to Harper and Hope, knowing that Kate would respond quickly to the 911 call.

"Congressman," I said amiably. "You just told Terry to shoot me."

"The hell I did, I told him to give you the gun."

"So you say, but your camera will tell the tale. Sit *still*, Jackson." He was rising to his feet, probably going for the disks.

"You're done, Congressman. So are you, Hope. That gun will put all three of you away for a long time."

"You won't make it stick, Starke. I didn't kill anybody."

"No you didn't. But he did." I nodded at Hamlin.

"What if he did? You can't prove I had anything to do with any of it. It's just a file. You can't tie it to me."

"Oh we can, but even if we can't—*he* can." I nodded in Hope's direction. "And he will. I already have him for money laundering. His name is on the spreadsheet as an authorized user, and as the last person to amend and save it."

Hope glared at me, his eyes glittering with hate.

"That being so, Jackson, I'm sure the Feds will cut you a deal. All you'll need to do is hand them your boss. Better ten years for money laundering—maybe only five if you're a good boy and cooperate... hell, maybe even immunity—than life without parole for conspiracy to murder, right?" I grinned at him. *Where the hell was Kate and her team?*

"You, Terry." I turned toward him, but I didn't think he could hear me; it looked like he'd gone into shock. I continued anyway. "You're done. I hope it was worth it."

It was at that moment that the cavalry arrived. Kate burst in, followed by Lonnie and a half-dozen uniforms, guns drawn.

"We got it all, Harry," Kate said, as we watched them cuff Hope and Little Billy. "You got them."

"You need to lock this place down, Kate. There's a camera, up there in the bookshelf. It's recording everything. My 911 call gave you probable cause to enter the office; it's a slam-dunk. I talked to Judge Strange before I left the office. He has a search warrant already signed and waiting for you, if you need it. You can legally grab the camera and recorder and the disks. It should have recorded everything that happened here. It will also prove that I had to shoot Hamlin in self-defense. No one can argue with Harper's own recordings. All you need do is find them.

"You don't really need the recordings I made, Kate. They're a bonus. It was never my plan to use them, not unless I had it all wrong. I suspected from day one that Harper had his office bugged. I planned to use Harper's own recordings against him. How to enable you to get your hands on them legally was the big problem. I had no idea how to do that, so I had to improvise a little. I knew Terry, his receptionist, was his man, and probably the killer too, but I couldn't prove that either. When Harper summoned him into the office, I knew I had them all. The fact that Harper told him to kill me, and that I had to shoot him, hence the 911 call, was all an unexpected bonus. I was lucky, I guess."

"You always are, Harry. But one day your luck's going to run out, and that's a day I never want to see. Give me your weapon and go wait for me in the car. Lonnie, go with him. Get out of here, Harry. I'll finish this up." She turned away, barely looking at me.

So, I thought, *it really is over.*

35

I drove slowly up Lookout Mountain early that afternoon. It was one of those days when all is well with the world. The rain had stopped, the sun was shining, the sky was clear and blue, and the view over downtown Chattanooga was stunning. Dr. Willard was waiting for me. We sat together in his living room and I told him the story, all of it except for Tabitha's so-called career. I just didn't see any point in destroying the man's illusions.

"So it's over, Doctor. Tabitha was a victim of corruption in high places. Because Falk gave her the files, she fell victim to Congressman Harper's political ambitions. I didn't use the whole retainer. Here's my invoice, marked as paid in full, and a check for the balance."

He took the check from me and tore it up, thanked me, then got up, patting me on the shoulder as he walked out of the room. I left his home and walked out into the bright sunshine, but it did little to uplift my spirits. Dr. Willard was a changed man, a sad old man who would have to live with the loss of his eldest daughter for the rest of his life. It was tough to take.

I drove back to the office. There was a message for me to call Kate, but somehow even that didn't make me feel any better. I dialed her anyway.

"Harry?"

"Yes. It's me. What's up?"

"What's wrong, Harry? You sound down in the dumps."

"Yeah, well, I've just got back from seeing Dr. Willard. Not a pleasant experience."

"Well, maybe this will cheer you up. We found it, the camera and the recorder, and a whole library of DVDs. Talk about Richard Nixon. He recorded everything. We even have Falk at his computer. The Feds will have a field day with it all. Oh, and you were right. There will be no charges for the shooting. It was self-defense, clear and simple. It's on camera. You're good; you're in the clear."

Good? The hell I am.

"How is he? Hamlin, I mean."

"He'll recover. He's at Erlanger, under guard. The Feds will transfer him to a government facility as soon as he's fit to move."

"How about Harper and Hope? Where are they?"

"In Federal custody, facing a litany of charges including conspiracy to commit murder. Hope was just a minor player, Harper's gofer. He'll probably cut a deal with the Feds. I doubt he'll do much time, if any. If he agrees to roll over on Harper... Harper and Hamlin will get life, if they're found guilty, and there's little doubt of that. You did good, Harry."

"Hah." I should have been elated, but somehow I wasn't. Not at all.

"The Mystica organization," she said, "has collapsed.

Shady Tree has disappeared. Gone south with his money, probably to the islands, but the Feds will get him, eventually. We grabbed his two boys, Stimpy and Ren, as you call them, but we had to let them go. They didn't know anything. So, it's done. Over. Good work, Harry."

Yeah, it's over. It's all over.

"Thanks. I guess we'll..."

"Yes, we'll talk, sometime. I'll call you. Goodbye, Harry." She disconnected before I could answer. I heaved a sigh, got myself a cup of coffee, and sat down again.

It was late when I finally decided that enough was enough. I was home by nine. It had been one hell of a day. I slept like the dead that night.

36

It was almost one o'clock the next afternoon when I picked Linda up at the airport, courtesy of my father and his Lear. We went to my condo on the river.

"Nice place, Harry."

I nodded. "I need to get something else. Someplace more private." I looked out through the kitchen window and nodded at the black Cadillac parked across the street. It was now on permanent lease to the Secret Service. "They'll give the place a bad name."

She laughed. It was more a gurgle than a laugh, but I loved it.

We ate a light lunch, drank two cups of coffee, and then sat together on the couch overlooking the river. It was raining again. The surface of the water was flat, and the raindrops turned it into an undulating bed of nails.

"So tell me all about it," she said.

I smiled a little. "Tell you about what?"

"Congressman Harper, silly."

"The PD arrested them all. Turned them over to the Feds. It's over."

"I know, but..."

So I told her. At least I told her what I thought she needed to know.

"Mystica was his honey trap. It was set up to attract the weak, and the rich and famous. It was all about power. Harper was picky about who he invited. He employed a number of people who worked as practitioners at OM, including Tabitha Willard and Terry Hamlin. Hamlin was a plant, though. He handled black ops for Harper. One of the regular practitioners handed your name to Harper; enter Terry Hamlin. To Harper, you were a gift from the gods, the pot of gold at the end of the rainbow. Or so he thought."

I took a sip of coffee, stared out over the rippled water, conscious that she was gazing up at me.

"The funny part of it is," I continued, "he didn't need Mystica. He was wealthy beyond most men's dreams. His financial empire was both vast and, for the most part, secret. It was all about power.

"I went to see Dr. Willard yesterday," I continued. "I let him down as gently as possible. No one other than my staff and Kate knows what Tabitha was really doing. There was no sense in destroying the man any more than he already was. Tabitha had already done that when she threw herself off the bridge.

"She was a Mystica practitioner with benefits. Clients could call the number on the card and book a session with her. She had access to one of the suites at the mall. She was, in fact, little more than an expensive hooker. She earned a lot of money and was allowed to keep it all. All she had to do was deliver the goods, her clients, to Harper.

"Michael Falk was in love with her. He knew what she was doing, and I think that when he stole the files he was trying to help her. He knew too much about Harper's business, and especially Harper's involvement with Mystica, but it was the theft of the Excel files that got him killed. I think he wanted to use them to put pressure on Harper, but it didn't work. As far as Harper was concerned, Tabitha was guilty by association. What Falk knew, she must know, too. He also wanted to recover the files. He had to make sure they didn't fall into the wrong hands, so he had Shady put his two mechanics onto her. Her meeting with Stimpy and Ren frightened her. And then, bless her, she bumped into me..."

"What's the matter, Harry? You don't look well."

"Oh, I'm okay. It's just that... well, it's my fault. She saw me on the bridge that night, and with the way I was dressed, she must have thought I was waiting for her, and she panicked and jumped."

"You can't blame yourself for that, Harry. You were just—"

"In the wrong place at the wrong time. I know. I realize that, but it doesn't help."

"What about the other girl?"

"Charlie? She was different. She wasn't involved with Mystica at all. I don't think she knew that Tabitha was either, just that she was into something different. She was a very smart girl... She was actually a man, you know. But smart as she was, she wasn't able to beat Harper."

"What went wrong?"

"Tabitha got scared and handed the drive to Charlie, then Tabitha threw Charlie under the bus with James and Gold. Harper sent Terry Hamlin to fix the problem, to recover the thumb drive, which he did, but not before Charlie copied and encrypted the files. They were her insurance. She thought they would save her life, and they might have if she'd been able to communicate her intentions to Harper, but Hamlin killed her before she could." I paused, thinking about poor Charlie.

"Go on, Harry."

"Well, as I said, Charlie was smart, but not smart enough. She must have thought she was in control, that she could stop the e-mails to me any time she wanted, and reschedule them if need be, but Hamlin killed her, and the e-mails went out on schedule, and that was the beginning of the end for Harper."

"What about the Hansen woman? Who killed her? And why?"

"That was another of Harper's mistakes. She was killed simply because of her interest in me. Terry had been following me. She was just another loose end that needed to be tidied up."

"What about Kate?"

I turned and smiled at her. "What about her?"

"Well, you two were an item for a very long time."

"And there's the problem. It was too long. It was nice—no, it was wonderful—but it wasn't going anywhere. We'll stay friends if she'll let me, but after all that's happened these last three weeks, that's all it can ever be. Our time together... is over."

She was quiet for several minutes. I knew she was mulling it over. Then she turned and looked at me. "Did you mean what you said about looking for another place?"

"I did. You need somewhere to get away, and the suite at the mall is no longer an option. I want to provide it."

"Harry. I'm fifty-two years old. I'm ten years older than you."

"Hah, you think that's a problem? My father's wife, his second, is almost twenty years younger than he is. Age is just a number. Look, Linda, you are one of the most powerful women in the world. Hell, you may be *the* most powerful one day."

She smiled and shook her head.

"Me, I'm just a Southern boy in a small Southern town. I enjoy what I do. Like you said, I'm forty-two years old. I don't intend to change my ways; I am what I am. You have a very busy life, and a very public one. You need a place where you can relax, let your hair down, be yourself now and then. Your public persona isn't really who you are; I know that. So, if you'll let me, I'd like to provide that place. And, Linda, I also want you in my life, if you'll have me."

"Sounds good to me. Now, tell me why you want me in your life."

The sun was just beginning to dip below the crest of Lookout Mountain. The sky was ablaze, a riot of red, gold, and purple. I leaned on the rail and looked down at the quiet waters of the Tennessee, thinking about the events of the past several weeks: the ups, the downs, the regrets—mostly the regrets. I must have been there for twenty minutes or more before I finally shook myself out of my reverie. I took Tabitha's pendant from my pocket, looked at it one last time, then tossed it over the rail. I watched it fall, spinning, glittering in the fading sunlight.

"Goodbye, Tabitha. Rest in peace."

THANK YOU

You finished it. Yay!

What did you think of it? Did you like it?

I hope you enjoyed reading Harry Starke as much as I did writing it. If you did, perhaps you'd like to read book 2 in the series, Two for the Money.

If you have comments or questions, you can contact me by e-mail at blair@blairhoward.com, and you can visit my website http://www.blairhoward.com.

Made in the USA
Monee, IL
30 June 2023

2bed11b5-fa1d-4c1b-a9fd-f4b2aabb80ffR01